A Happy Death

Alex Telman

Published by Alex Telman, 2024.

This is a work of fiction. Similarities to real people, places, or events are entirely coincidental.

A HAPPY DEATH

First edition. December 24, 2024.

ISBN: 979-8227894670

Written by Alex Telman.

Table of Contents

Author's Note

Dear Reader,

This book is not for everyone. It wasn't meant to be. It's for the broken, the discarded, the invisible people who keep slipping through the cracks of a world that pretends to care. It's for those who find themselves on the edge, looking in at a life that feels like a mirage, a distant dream that's forever out of reach.

A Happy Death is a story about the people we walk past every day—the ones whose names we don't know, whose faces we've forgotten, whose stories we've never bothered to hear. It's about Dez, a man who lost himself somewhere between the cracks in the system, a casualty of a world that doesn't have room for the broken or the lost. His is the story of a man who had dreams but was suffocated by the weight of a world that only values what can be monetized, what can be made productive. And yet, despite all the injustice and despair, Dez's story is not a tragedy. It's an existential reflection, a journey into the heart of what it means to live in a world that offers no easy answers.

The city, in this story, is not a backdrop—it's a character, a brutal machine that chews up and spits out the lives of those it deems expendable. I wrote this book because the city is indifferent. It moves forward with or without you, and for many, it moves on after swallowing them whole. New York is a place of contradictions—dreams are born here, but so are nightmares. And in those forgotten corners, in the alleyways and the subways, in the places where the sun never seems to shine, lives like Dez's are lived and lost.

This story is a meditation on alienation, on the existential struggle of a life that doesn't matter to anyone except the person living it. It's about the kind of person the world would rather forget—the homeless, the marginalized, the underclass. We see them on the streets, but we don't see them. We see the shadows of lives that could have been, but we don't take the time to wonder what happened, what went wrong. The truth is, we don't care, and this story is an attempt to ask why.

I've spent years walking the streets of cities like New York, watching people lose themselves, watching people be swallowed by the same system that promises so much and delivers so little. And I've always wondered about the lives behind the faces we ignore. Who are they? What made them disappear? What would have happened if they hadn't fallen through the cracks? And most importantly, what happens to them once they're gone?

This is a story about failure, but not in the way most people think of failure. It's not about the kind of failure that can be fixed, the kind that comes with a second chance. This is the failure of a world that doesn't leave space for second chances. It's the kind of failure that starts long before a person hits rock bottom. It's the failure of the system, of society, of the unspoken contract we all live by—the one that says if you work hard enough, if you play by the rules, you'll make it. The truth is, some people never even get the chance to try.

And yet, Dez's story is also about something else: the quiet dignity that can exist in the face of absolute defeat. In his final days, Dez does not beg for sympathy. He doesn't ask for understanding. He doesn't even ask for anything. He simply exists, in the way that only someone who has nothing left to lose can. There is a strange freedom in that, a clarity of vision that the rest of us, wrapped up in our privileges and distractions, often miss.

But this book is not just about Dez. It's about all of us. It's about the choices we make and the choices we don't. It's about the lives we fail to live, the connections we don't make, and the systems we fail to dismantle. Dez's death is not just his. It's all of ours.

I wrote this book to tell the story of a man who could have been anything, but wasn't. Who could have mattered, but didn't. It's a story about the cruelty of a system that rewards the lucky and punishes the unlucky. It's about all the lives lived in the margins, lives that go unnoticed, lives that fade into the background, lives that are never remembered.

In the end, it's a story about what we are willing to forget—and what we choose to remember. The question is, will we remember? Or will we simply move on to the next headline, the next story, the next life that will be forgotten as quickly as the one before it?

This is Dez's story, but it's also the story of all of us. And if we're lucky, maybe it's a wake-up call we'll hear before it's too late.

Introduction

You're not going to find any redemption in these pages. There's no happy ending, no heroic struggle against the odds. What you'll find instead is a life worn raw by the streets, a soul broken and battered by the city that doesn't care. This is a story about Dez, a man who learned the hard way that life doesn't care about your dreams, your past, or your potential. It swallows you whole, chews you up, and spits you out without so much as a shrug.

Dez wasn't always homeless. He had a name, a history, and someone who once loved him. He was a young man with ideas and hopes, standing on the edge of something, waiting for life to mean something more. But the system doesn't care about the ones at the edges. It doesn't notice when people fall through the cracks. And so Dez found himself sprawled on the hard, unforgiving pavement of New York, his body just another casualty in the endless cycle of poverty, neglect, and indifference.

There are no angels here. No saviors. Just the raw pulse of a city that never sleeps, never stops, and never looks back. This is a story that smells like piss and burnt coffee, sounds like the endless hum of subway trains and distant sirens, and tastes like the bitterness of cheap whiskey and failure. It's a story of struggle, but not the kind of struggle that gets celebrated. This is the kind of struggle that gets swept into the shadows and forgotten—except by the people who live it, who breathe it, who die in it.

Through Dez's eyes, we'll see New York not as a bright, flashing beacon of possibility, but as a machine—cold, efficient, and indifferent. It doesn't care if you rise to the top or fall to the bottom. The city doesn't owe you anything. You can grind your bones against its streets, and it won't even flinch. The world moves forward with or without you. And it'll forget you just as quickly.

But Dez won't be forgotten here. He is a voice for the voiceless, a face in the crowd that no one ever really sees, a life that never mattered to the people who walk past him every day. And yet, in the moments before he disappears, we glimpse the quiet tragedy of a man who could have been something more—if the world hadn't broken him first.

This is a novel about alienation, about the failure of systems, and about the terrible indifference of life itself. It's an invitation to sit with the uncomfortable truth that, sometimes, death is the only release from a world that demands too much and gives too little.

But don't expect a neat conclusion. Expect no easy answers. Expect only what Dez gets—raw, unflinching truth.

Welcome to A Happy Death. It's a place where the dead still have stories to tell, even if the world won't listen.

Chapter 1. Introduction to Dez

The City in the Dark

The city never sleeps, but it never gives a damn, either.

I lie here, pressed against the rough stone of this doorway, trying to keep some part of me warm. The rain is relentless, falling in sheets that sting when they hit my skin. But what's pain anymore? My body's gone numb. It's not the rain that keeps me awake. It's the noise. Always the noise.

Car tires screech. The hum of distant conversations. The clatter of a thousand lives that don't know I'm here, crumpled against the building like a discarded cigarette. I'm invisible, yet here I am, alive enough to feel every wet breath, every gust of wind that cuts through the thin fabric of my jacket. People walk by, wrapped in their own little worlds, heads down, eyes glazed over, walking past me as if I don't exist. I'm nothing.

Sometimes I think that's the point of New York. To become part of its backdrop. The city devours you, chews you up and spits you out like gum on the sidewalk, but it never stops moving. I'm nothing but a blotch of gray against the mosaic of human suffering. They step over me without blinking. And I don't even blame them. Hell, I can't blame anyone anymore.

What's the point of blaming? It's all just part of the machinery. We're all cogs in it, grinding away until we snap.

It's been years since I first ended up here, years since the world made any sense. I was never a kid who dreamt of a life on the street. Hell, who dreams of this? You don't hear about the ones who fall off, the ones who disappear into the cracks of society, swallowed whole. It doesn't make for good TV. But here I am.

You only hear about the ones who make it. The ones who climb to the top, look down, and forget about us. The ones who leave people like me to rot in the shadows. And yet, here I am.

A HAPPY DEATH

I pull my knees tighter into my chest, hoping to keep the cold from gnawing through the little warmth left in my bones. I should sleep, but my mind is a furnace, too hot, too busy. The past spins like a record stuck on repeat—faces, names, all of it blurring together in the dark. Ana's face, especially. I haven't seen her in years, but her face is still so damn clear. She used to smile like the sun, and I used to think maybe, just maybe, that could save me.

But who was I fooling? I couldn't even save myself. The drinking, the endless numbness—it kept me from feeling the truth: that I wasn't enough. Not for her. Not for anyone. The only thing I've been good at is survival. But survival's a shitty goal. Survival's a joke. It's not a life. It's just a holding pattern, a circling of the drain.

The rain turns into something softer, almost peaceful. But peace is also a joke. I haven't felt peace since before I lost everything. Back when I still had hope. Before I was nothing. Back when I thought I was worthy of saving.

I watch a couple pass by, laughing. They're young. They don't see me, don't even register that I exist. Their joy stings, sharp and bitter. I wonder what it's like to not be invisible. To have someone care. To have something to fight for.

The man laughs louder, and the woman punches him playfully in the arm. I can't help it. I hate them for it. That kind of happiness doesn't exist for people like me. It's a different world. A world I'm no longer a part of, if I ever was.

I catch a glimpse of my reflection in the shop window across the street. My face is haggard, skin pulled tight over bones. My eyes are red and tired, but not from sleep. From something deeper. It's like I can see all the years of hard living etched into my face. I don't recognize the person staring back at me, but I've been staring at him for so long that I can't tell where I end and he begins. Maybe we're the same. Maybe we've always been the same.

I don't know what I'm doing anymore. I'm just here. Surviving. But is that even enough? Is that what it means to live?

A car honks, a siren wails, someone shouts in the distance. Life keeps on moving. The city keeps on spinning. But I'm stuck. Stuck in this same moment, every moment. The rain keeps falling, cold as the world that forgot me.

The world doesn't care about people like me. The city doesn't care. Hell, I barely care about myself anymore. But maybe that's the point. Maybe caring only drags you deeper into this cesspool of humanity. Maybe it's better to just let go. To stop giving a damn. To just be numb to it all.

But then, out of the corner of my eye, I see her.

She's standing by the corner, holding a thermos. She doesn't look at me, doesn't acknowledge me at first. But then, she does. She looks right at me, and for a second, the whole world falls silent. She's young, mid-twenties maybe, wearing a scarf around her neck like she's trying to hide from the cold. I don't know what it is about her—maybe it's the way her eyes aren't glazed over, like most people's are. She looks at me like I matter.

I can't take it. My heart gives a quick, erratic beat, and I want to turn away. I want to pretend I didn't see her. But I don't.

"Coffee?" she asks, her voice soft, almost hesitant. Her hand is outstretched, offering warmth. Offering something I've long forgotten how to accept.

I should say no. I should turn her away. I don't deserve her kindness.

But instead, I find myself reaching for it. The warmth. I feel the weight of the thermos in my hands, the steam rising. I drink. I don't think about it. I just drink.

We don't speak. She watches me for a moment, and then without a word, she turns and walks away, disappearing into the night.

The coffee tastes bitter, but it's the sweetest thing I've had in a long time.

And for the first time in a long time, I feel something—something that isn't numbness. Something like hope, or maybe just the smallest crack of human connection. I hate myself for needing it, but I take it anyway. And then, I'm left alone again.

But maybe that's the point. The city doesn't care. But once in a while, someone does.

Survival at All Costs

I can't escape the sound of the city, no matter how far I shove my head into the corner of this rotting cardboard. It's the noise of a hundred thousand people fighting to survive, and yet nobody's winning. It just keeps moving, a machine with too many gears. Every honk, every siren, every footstep echoes down my spine like a threat. I used to sleep through it, block it out with a bottle or a needle. But now it's just a soundtrack to my misery, a relentless reminder that I'm still here.

The city doesn't care. It never did. It was always too big for me, too loud, too bright. When I was younger, I thought I could make something of myself here, like the stories said. You know, the ones about making it big, escaping the cage. But here I am, thirty, huddled beneath this awning, the rain turning the sidewalk into a slick mess. Nothing but a ghost. Nothing but a shadow of a person.

Survival's all I've got left. Survival and shame.

I used to think I could break free. Thought maybe if I just found the right angle, the right connection, something would change. But survival's the only thing I can trust now. There's no love left in me, no dreams. Just scraping by, day to day, hour to hour, in the same damn city I thought would save me. Only difference now is I know better.

It's funny how people think the streets are all about drugs and alcohol. That's just the beginning. After that, you start learning how to survive, how to avoid the cracks in the pavement that'll swallow you whole. How to make the city your enemy, but also your ally. People are just ghosts here, and they can't see you. They don't want to. They never did. You become a part of the background noise.

I keep my head low, my eyes on the ground. I've learned not to make eye contact. Eye contact is an invitation for trouble. Some asshole with a badge sees you in their line of sight and thinks they've got the right to break your back. So you keep your head low, and when you do look up, you make sure you're not seen. Just like everyone else in this godforsaken place.

Sometimes, I can feel myself turning into them—the ones I hated when I first came here. The ones who've given up, lost all hope. I can see it in their eyes when I pass them on the corner. The glassy look, the permanent cloud of indifference. Like they've been left outside for too long, soaking up the filth of this city until it's all they are. I don't want to become that. But I'm getting close. Too close.

I haven't seen Frank in days. He's probably holed up somewhere, trying to ride out another bender or hiding from the cops. I don't know why I even care anymore. Frank's the guy who told me all the ugly truths about street life. Told me about the scams, the thieves, the animals who'll cut you open for a dime. He's the one who taught me how to beg, how to take what I need, no matter who I have to hurt in the process.

I don't know if I can live like that anymore. Not that I've got anything to live for, but I still remember what it felt like before. Before I lost everything. Before the booze became my only friend. Before the streets carved a hole in me so deep, I didn't know how to fill it anymore.

The thing about survival is that it makes you numb. Numb to the cold, to the hunger, to the pain. It's the slow death of your humanity, one scrape at a time. It's like you're walking through a fog, and you can't remember what you're doing or why you're doing it. All you know is that you're still breathing, still moving, and that's supposed to be enough. But it isn't. Not for me, anyway.

Marie still comes by sometimes, brings me a cup of coffee or a sandwich. She keeps telling me there's hope, that there's a way out. I just laugh. She's trying to fix me, but you can't fix something that's already broken. I told her once that the world was broken, and I was just its product. She didn't like that. She tried to tell me that I had potential, that I could make something of myself if I wanted to. But that's the problem with people like her—they never see the bottom. They see the idea of you, not the reality.

I used to care what people thought. I used to dream of getting out, of finding a way out of this mess. But now I'm just here, in this corner of New York, where nothing matters. Nothing but survival. I don't even remember the last time I felt anything other than cold or hunger. And when I do feel something, it's just a reminder that I can't have it.

I don't know how much longer I'll last. Every day's a countdown. I'm just waiting for the end, like everyone else. I don't know if I'll die out here or if I'll just fade away slowly, like the rest of the ghosts on the street. Maybe the rain will drown me, or maybe I'll just stop breathing one night, and nobody will notice. I don't care either way. I don't even know if I'm still alive, really. I just know that I'm here. Still here. Just trying to survive.

Survival at all costs. But at what cost?

The Concept of Death

I wake to the sound of rain tapping against the plastic sheets of my makeshift shelter, that sick, monotonous drumming that echoes down my spine and rattles my bones. It's not the rain that's so damned bad, it's the cold. It doesn't just freeze you—it fills you up with that bitter emptiness, like the whole city is nothing more than a hollow shell that I've been shoved into. The city doesn't care, doesn't even notice. There's a part of me that wishes it would just collapse, let the whole fucking thing fall apart. It's like the best part of me is already gone, already disappeared into the cracks, the shadows of this wasteland.

But I'm still here, aren't I? Alive. Barely. I twist my body into a better position, trying to find some warmth in this dirty corner. The sound of the traffic hums in the background, a low, ugly growl that never stops. Like the city is some kind of machine grinding people down, chewing them up, spitting them out. The folks on the other side, the ones who don't even see us anymore, they're just cogs in the wheel, too—pushing, pulling, trying to get to the top. The thing is, most of them don't even know it's a fucking rat race. They just keep running, don't they? For what? Some apartment in a building where the walls are so thin you can hear the guy above you jerking off? A shitty job that doesn't even pay for half your rent? It's all the same.

The rain's heavier now, and I close my eyes. I can't shake the thought of death. Not like it's some distant, abstract thing anymore, something to be feared or even longed for. No, it's right here with me—breathing the same stale air, filling my lungs with every breath. There's no mystery to it. It's not some grand event. It's just another step in the process. I think of it like peeling an onion. You shed one layer, and you get to the next, until it's all gone, and you're left with nothing but skin and emptiness. It's peaceful. There's peace in it.

Maybe that's the joke. You spend your whole life trying to escape it, fighting to stay alive, to survive, but all the while, you're walking toward it. You're already halfway there, and you don't even know it. And me? Well, I've known it for a long time. There was a time I thought I could fight it—fix myself, get clean, go back to Ana, back to a real life. But what's left of that? What's left of anything?

I think of the people I used to know. The ones who made promises, who tried to save me, like Marie. She was the first one who ever looked at me and saw something more than just the dirt on my face, the stench of piss on my clothes. She was full of light, like the sunlight on a spring morning when everything feels like it might be okay, if only for a moment. She had this idea, you know? That there was something worth saving in me. She'd bring me food, try to get me to come with her to one of those shelters where they hand you a shitty bed and a blanket that smells like mold. I'd listen to her and smile, but I couldn't get out of my head. The weight of the city on my shoulders, the bitterness in my chest. I didn't even know if I wanted to survive anymore.

Survival, that's the thing. It's all you can do when you've got nothing. You fight, scrape, beg, steal, but in the end, all you've really got is the desperate, gnawing need to breathe. And that's it. That's the whole game. I see the people on the streets, just like me, living day to day like it's some kind of contest to see who can last the longest. We're all fighting for something, but we're not sure what. There's no prize. No finish line. Just the slow, aching march of time. And the city keeps moving—fast, indifferent, like a beast that's never going to stop hunting, never going to let you go. You're just another mouth to feed, another body to step over.

I can feel the ache in my bones, the weight of it all. The longer I stay, the more I feel like I'm just fading into the background, becoming a shadow of myself. I'm a statistic now, part of the noise. But that's what it is, isn't it? All of us out here, in the gutters and alleys, we're just statistics in a city that only cares about the numbers. How many are out there? How many have made it to the shelters? How many have died? They don't care about our names, our stories. They don't care about the fact that once, we were someone. Maybe not much, but we mattered.

So why keep fighting? I could die tomorrow, or I could die next year. What's the difference? It's all the same, isn't it? The end is just the end. And I'm not scared anymore. The city can do what it wants. It can chew me up, spit me out, leave me lying in a gutter to rot. I don't care. Maybe it'll be easier than all this. Maybe death's the only thing that can free me from the constant grind.

There was a time when I thought I was going to fix it. That I was going to climb out of this shit hole, maybe meet someone like Ana again, clean myself up, get a job. But that was a joke. You can't climb out of a hole if you don't have a ladder, and you sure as hell can't pull yourself up by your bootstraps when your boots have been stolen and you're too damn tired to even move. No, that's not the way out.

And what about the rest of the world? The ones who live on the other side? The ones who never see us, who just walk by, pretending we don't exist? They've got their lives, their dreams, their bullshit. They've got their shiny cars and their office jobs, and they don't see the rest of us, the ones who've slipped through the cracks. They don't want to. It's easier to pretend we don't exist, to act like we're not here, like we're nothing but background noise. But we're here. And one day, one of them might realize just how close they are to being us.

But not today.

Today, I'll just wait for the rain to stop. Or maybe I won't. Maybe I'll just lie here, in the dark, and wait for the peace to come. Because, in the end, it's all the same. Just another layer peeled away, another day gone.

Chapter 2: The Streets of New York

The Vultures and the Strays

I move through the streets like I don't exist. The city doesn't care about me, doesn't even notice I'm here. I'm just another ghost in the gutter, dodging cars and people wrapped up in their own shiny, fake worlds. They don't see me. They don't want to. They've got their phones, their money, their fake smiles to protect them. The city's a beast, hungry for the weak, and I'm just another carcass it's chewing up, spitting out.

The sidewalk is a stage for the usual cast—bums, drunks, broken souls who didn't make it. They sit, they wait, their eyes too wide for what they've seen, staring at nothing, like they're waiting for the city to finally swallow them whole. I nod as I pass them—ghosts in the same damn cemetery—and they nod back. No words, just empty gestures, the kind that mean nothing and everything all at once.

On the corner, there's a woman with a cardboard sign, her clothes somehow still pressed, her hands still clean. "Anything helps," the sign says. But we both know the game. She's playing, pretending like she hasn't already been chewed up by this city, this cold, unforgiving machine. Her poverty is the product of a system that packages suffering, wraps it in neat bows and sells it as charity. I don't give her anything. I don't have anything to give, and she doesn't deserve it. She's one of the vultures, picking at the scraps of a life she thought she could have.

I keep moving. The stench of piss is thick here, hanging in the air like a bad memory. Hot garbage, burnt plastic, rot and sweat mixing together in a thick stew. It clings to me, but it's nothing new. I've worn this smell too long to care anymore. It's the city's scent. It's my scent. We're both drenched in it.

A kid walks by, his fancy jacket too big for him, earbuds jammed in his ears like he's trying to shut out the real world. His face says it all: the world belongs to him, daddy's money will save him. He doesn't even glance at me, doesn't even see me. He's in his bubble, and it's so thick it might just protect him. But maybe one day, it'll pop. Maybe one day he'll end up like me—forgotten, a stain on the sidewalk.

I want to shout at him, tell him how little he knows, but I don't. What's the point? He's not listening. Nobody listens to us—the ones who don't matter. We're just the background noise, the dead weight that makes this city real for the ones who matter. When they pass, we fade into the cracks, like dust on their shoes.

The sirens wail in the distance, the city's pulse. A dying animal's heartbeat, steady and unyielding. It's not for me. Not anymore. It's for the ones who get to go home to warm apartments, to have their teeth fixed and their bellies full, to get treated like they exist. They don't know what it's like to be invisible.

I walk into the park. A few strays sit on a bench, holding bottles like they're treasures. Bobby's one of them, the scraggly bastard who's been here longer than I have. His eyes flick over me, sizing me up, deciding if I'm still part of the pack or if I've crossed over to ghost territory. I've been here long enough to know the rules: nod, grunt, keep your distance. Survival's a solo sport.

"Hey, Dez," Bobby says, voice scratchy, shot through with years of smoke and whiskey. "Got a smoke?"

I dig into my pocket, pull out the last one. The last thing I've got to offer. I light it, and the orange glow flickers in the dark. It's not much, but it's mine. I hand it to Bobby, and he takes it without a word. A little exchange. No thanks, no promises.

Another guy, big and bloated with a patchy beard, watches from across the bench. "You got more?" he asks, his breath stinking of cheap whiskey.

"No," I say, voice flat. "You want a trick? Watch me disappear."

He laughs, but it's not a laugh. It's just a noise, hollow and empty, a sound that's been around too long. It's not joy. It's not even irony. It's just the sound of living with nothing left to lose.

The bottle gets passed around, and I take a swig. It burns, but it doesn't help. Nothing helps. Nothing changes. I keep breathing, keep waking up to this world that's already decided I'm not worth the time.

A woman walks by, heels clicking like she's in a hurry. She carries a coffee cup like it's a weapon. She doesn't see me. Doesn't see any of us. She's in her world, and we're in ours, but hers is the one that counts. Hers is the one that matters. She walks like she's already won, like the city's already given her what I had to steal. And I hate her for it.

But I won't say anything. I won't scream or throw my anger at her. It wouldn't make a difference. This city's a jungle, and I'm not the prey. I'm the carcass, picked clean, waiting to be forgotten.

The fat guy elbows me, breaking the silence. "You know, Dez, we're all just waiting to die. You're already halfway there."

I look at him—his yellowed teeth, his empty eyes—and for a moment, I almost laugh. Almost. Because he's right. We're all just waiting for the end. The problem isn't dying. The problem is living. The problem is surviving in a city that doesn't care whether you breathe or not. It doesn't matter. They want us to disappear. To blend into the background.

But not today. Not today. Maybe tomorrow, but not today. I'm not ready to give up my piece of this sidewalk. Not yet.

I finish the smoke, flick the butt onto the ground, and watch it burn. It's like me—slowly fading, burning out, but still here. Still struggling. Still alive.

For one sickening moment, I wonder if I'll ever stop fighting.

But I won't go down easy. Not today. Not yet. Maybe tomorrow, but not today.

Not while I'm still breathing. Not while I'm still alive.

The Invisible Ones

I wake up with the sun, though it doesn't feel like waking. It's just a new day, a new moment to be ignored, to scrape by, to shuffle through the motions. The city hums around me, indifferent as always. I don't bother with stretches, with prayers, with false hope. I roll out of the flattened cardboard that's been my mattress for months, maybe years, and get up.

The concrete greets me like a lover who's stopped caring. It doesn't say good morning, doesn't tell me to have a nice day. It just is. I walk down the street, past the same faces, the same garbage cans, the same ghosts that haunt this place. There's no ceremony in it, just the clack of my shoes against pavement, the rhythm of survival.

I stop at the corner and stare at the storefronts, the clean windows reflecting a world I don't belong to. Tourists walk by, clicking their cameras, smiling at things they think they understand. They're laughing, but not with me. Not at me either. I'm just part of the scenery, a fixture of the city like the cracked sidewalk or the bent lampposts. I can see them pretend they don't see me, some even smiling when they meet my eyes—like they're doing me a favor. Like they've been kind enough to acknowledge my existence, but only for a second, like a momentary curiosity.

I'm not even real to them. I'm a backdrop, part of the show.

One of them stops, a young woman with blonde hair and eyes that reflect too much innocence. She's clutching a designer bag, the kind of bag that costs more than my whole existence. She digs into her purse and pulls out a crumpled dollar bill. She hands it to me with a smile that's far too practiced, far too clean.

"Here," she says, "God bless."

She walks away, not even waiting for me to say thanks, or anything. I'm nothing but a transaction to her. A line on the ledger of her life, one of those little good deeds people collect to make themselves feel better.

I stare at the dollar for a moment, then crumple it up and shove it in my pocket. It means nothing. Not even enough to buy a warm drink, but it's the price of my humanity, or what's left of it. The exchange is hollow. She moves on, as she should. She'll go back to her world, and I'll stay here, with the rest of the ghosts.

The streets are filled with them. The invisible ones. The ones who walk through life unnoticed, discarded by the system, by the rules that say you need a place to live, an ID, a job, a future. None of us have that. We're just drifting, waiting for the city to spit us out or swallow us whole.

I see the same faces every day—broken people, empty-eyed, their bodies like skeletons wrapped in filthy rags. They beg, they shout, they sit in doorways with their hands out, offering a smile that's just as hollow as mine. They all know. We know. We're invisible. We are a footnote in someone's forgotten story, a speck of dust in the corner of a glass case.

I stop at a trash can, hoping for something edible. There's a half-eaten sandwich in a plastic bag, some stale chips, and a bottle of warm soda. I pick it out carefully, like I'm handling the last treasure on Earth. I'm not picky anymore. I've learned not to be. My stomach's used to whatever comes its way. If it's food, it'll do. If it's not, then I'll learn to survive without.

I eat quickly, hoping no one will stop to watch. They never do, though. They never look down. They just keep walking, eyes forward, as if they can't see us—the ones sitting in the gutters, the ones begging for scraps of the life they take for granted.

A man in a business suit walks by, his face a mask of purpose. He doesn't even flinch when he sees me. His eyes stay locked ahead, just another person who's learned to ignore the pain around him. He doesn't even know I'm here. And why should he? I'm invisible to him, just like I am to everyone else. I might as well be part of the air he's breathing, just something that passes in and out without mattering.

It doesn't matter.

I watch him disappear into the crowd, swallowed by the masses. I feel a pang of something, but I can't name it. Not anger, not resentment—not exactly. It's something deeper, a kind of hollow emptiness that presses in on me every time

I realize that I'm not even a ghost. I'm a shadow without substance, flickering on the edges of their lives. I was once something, or at least I thought I was. But now? Now I'm a broken joke, an afterthought in a city that's too busy with its own problems to care about mine.

The tourists don't notice. They don't even stop for a second, not even for a picture of me. They'll snap photos of the skyline, the bridges, the landmarks. They'll leave with their happy memories and their Instagram filters, and I'll stay here. Waiting.

A group of them, young and full of energy, stop in front of me, laughing, their hands stuffed with overpriced coffees and bags of food they don't need. They look at me like I'm an exhibit at the zoo. I catch one of their eyes, and she smiles—a pitying smile, as if I'm some tragic figure she feels sorry for but won't ever help. She says something to her friends, and they all laugh, but not at me—no, it's not even about me. I'm a sideshow, a decoration to their perfect little day.

I turn away, back to the sidewalk, back to the next block, the next corner. The next empty feeling.

The truth is, there's nothing left in me to give, no kindness to return. All I have is survival. I'm not here for the pity, for the dollar bills, for the scraps. I'm here because I'm still breathing, and that's the only victory I can claim anymore. It's not much, but it's mine.

I head down to the park where the others are. Bobby's there, drunk as usual. He's sitting with his back against a tree, eyes glazed over like he's seeing something far away, like he's already gone. I nod to him, but he doesn't look up. He's lost in his own shit, just like the rest of us.

A man walks past and shakes his head as he sees Bobby—disgusted, like he's seen the worst of humanity. He doesn't even slow down, just keeps walking, his footsteps a beat to the soundtrack of a world that doesn't give a damn. And that's fine. It's just the way it is.

I lean back against the tree, my legs tired, my mind empty. I can hear the city moving around me, its pulse, its hum. But none of it matters. We're the forgotten ones. The invisible ones. And we'll stay here until we're gone.

Despair and Defiance

The night creeps in like a bad memory, one you can't shake off no matter how hard you try. The city wears its darkness like a badge of honor, as if it's proud of the filth that gathers in its corners after the sun goes down. The lights in the buildings above me flicker, their glow mocking me, like the world is saying, Here's your city. Here's your future. And it's a fuckin' shadow, Dez. Just a shadow.

I'm sitting on the same bench where I always sit, watching the people rush by, their lives flashing in front of me like they're all in a hurry to be somewhere important, somewhere better. They pass without even knowing I exist, like I'm a forgotten footnote in a book that no one's reading anymore. I don't know why I bother watching them. Maybe it's just a way to remind myself that I'm still here, still alive, still part of the world, even though the world doesn't know I'm here.

I can hear the hum of the city, its pulse, its heartbeat. It's like a fevered engine running on fumes, and I'm just a part of the background noise—the forgotten static between the important signals. A train passes in the distance, its rumble shaking the ground beneath me. It's a sound I've learned to ignore, but tonight, it feels like a reminder of something I've almost forgotten: that everything moves forward, except for me. I'm the one left behind. The one stuck in place, unable to escape the gravity of the streets.

There's a guy standing by the corner, his hands shaking as he counts the change in his pockets. He's wearing a nice suit, the kind of suit that costs more than I've made in my entire life. But he looks like he's just as lost as I am. I wonder if he ever feels it, that heavy weight of being alive, that feeling like the whole world is on your back and you can't take a step without being crushed by it.

I want to ask him if he's ever thought about what it means to be invisible. If he's ever felt like a ghost, floating through a world that doesn't care enough to even look in your direction. But I don't. I don't say anything. What's the point? People don't want to know. They don't want to see. They're too busy pretending that everything's okay, that their shiny suits and their fancy cars mean something. It's all a lie, but it's a lie they need to believe.

A woman walks past me, her heels clicking on the pavement, her face locked in that look of determination that only the rich can afford. She doesn't see me. Doesn't even glance in my direction. I watch her, her perfectly manicured hands clutching a shopping bag like it's a life raft. I wonder what she's going to buy. Another pair of shoes? Another bag to hang in the closet with all the others? I wonder if she knows what it's like to be hungry, to be cold, to have nothing but the concrete beneath you and the stars above you, mocking you for thinking they're there to help.

She doesn't look at me. No one ever does. I'm just a shadow in their world, a stain they can't see, a part of the background that they've learned to ignore.

But I can't help it. For a second, I let myself dream. I let myself think, Maybe there's still a chance. Maybe there's still a way out of this. Maybe one day, someone will see me, really see me, and offer me a hand, a way out of this endless cycle of nothing. I can almost taste it—the hope, that faint flicker of something better—but before it can even settle in my chest, the city swallows it up, and I'm left with nothing but the taste of ash.

I take a swig from the bottle of cheap whiskey I've been nursing. It burns like fire, but it's the only warmth I know. The streets are cold tonight, colder than usual. Maybe it's the wind, or maybe it's just the feeling that the world is closing in around me, tightening like a noose. The air smells like wet asphalt and sweat, a mixture of decay that's become as familiar to me as my own skin. The stench of desperation hangs in the air, thick and suffocating, and I wonder if it's always been here, or if it's just me who's changed.

I want to scream. I want to shout at the sky and demand an answer. I want to know why I'm still here, why I keep going when every instinct tells me to stop, to give up, to let go. But there's a part of me, deep down, that refuses to let go. Maybe it's pride, maybe it's something else, but I can't surrender. Not yet. Not while I'm still breathing.

I see another tourist. She's taking pictures of the city, snapping shots of the skyline as if it's a postcard. She's smiling, her face lit up with that same fake brightness that everyone in this city wears like a mask. I can tell she's not looking at me, not really. She's looking through me, the way everyone does. She's too busy capturing the perfect moment to see the mess behind it all, the decay, the rot, the people like me who don't fit into her perfect picture of the world.

I want to ask her if she knows what it's like to be invisible. If she knows what it's like to walk the streets and feel the weight of a thousand eyes on your back, all of them pretending they don't see you, pretending you don't exist. I want to scream, but I don't. I just sit there, in the cold, in the dark, and wait for the city to swallow me whole.

But as the night stretches on, something inside me refuses to die. Something refuses to let go. I don't know what it is, but it's there, flickering like a dying ember in the pit of my stomach. It's the one thing I've got left—the one thing I haven't given up on yet.

I know this city doesn't care about me. I know it's just waiting for me to disappear, to fade into the background like the rest of the forgotten souls who've come before me. But I'm not ready yet. Not today. Maybe tomorrow, but not today.

The whiskey burns again as I take another swallow, and for a brief moment, I let myself feel something—something like hope. Something like defiance. It's a fleeting thing, and I know it won't last, but for tonight, it's enough.

I flick the empty bottle to the side and stand up. The city's still here, still breathing, still indifferent. But so am I.

Chapter 3: The First Glimpse of Marie

Unexpected Kindness

I wake up to the usual ache, the one that tells me the night's done and it's time to drag my sorry ass back into another miserable day. The sun's already up, slicing through the trash-strewn streets, casting shadows on the faces of the desperate, the broken, the invisible. I'm just one more of them, another homeless bastard taking up space in a city that can't wait to shove me out of the way. The air smells like piss and car exhaust, and the city's heartbeat keeps pounding in my skull. I don't move right away, just lie there on my cardboard, waiting for something—anything—to make me feel alive. I don't know why I keep waiting. Maybe I'm just a creature of habit, clinging to the wreckage like it's all I have left.

Then I see her.

She's walking towards me like she's out for a stroll in the park, coffee in one hand, sandwich in the other. She's young, maybe early thirties, blonde hair tied back in a ponytail, face flushed from the cold or the early morning light, or maybe it's just the kind of look people wear when they still believe the world's good, when they haven't had it beaten out of them yet. She stops a few feet away, looks down at me, and smiles. I don't know how to respond to that. I'm not used to smiles, not from anyone who isn't trying to sell me something or lock me up.

"Hey," she says, her voice light, almost too cheerful. "I got you a coffee. And a sandwich. You hungry?"

I don't say anything right away. I'm too busy trying to figure out what her angle is. No one just walks up to a stranger, a homeless guy, and gives him coffee and food without wanting something in return. There's always a catch. A hidden price. People like her—they're too clean, too bright, too damn well-fed to just be handing out freebies on the street. I can smell her perfume now, something floral and fresh, like she's been living in a world far away from mine.

I don't trust her. Not one bit.

"Why're you doing this?" I ask, my voice rough from sleep and whiskey, like it hasn't been used in days. "You think I'm some charity case? Is this your feel-good moment for the day? Pat yourself on the back for being a 'good person' and move on to your next victim?"

She doesn't flinch. Doesn't back away. She just stands there, the coffee and sandwich still in her hands, looking at me like I'm a puzzle she's trying to solve.

"I'm just trying to help," she says, her words slower now, as if she's trying to keep me from snapping. "I thought you might be hungry. And it's cold out. You need something warm."

Her eyes meet mine, and for the first time in a long while, I feel something stir. It's not trust, no, I'm not that foolish. It's just—something that feels almost like a spark, like a match being struck in a dark room. For a second, I'm caught in that gaze, those eyes, and I'm not sure what I see there. Maybe it's pity. Maybe it's something else. Either way, it makes me uncomfortable.

"You think I need saving?" I ask, almost a whisper, but loud enough for her to hear. "I don't need your goddamn pity. Keep your sandwich, your coffee, your—whatever the hell you think you're doing—keep it."

She doesn't leave. She doesn't argue either. She just stands there like a goddamn saint, waiting for me to say something else. Waiting for me to take the damn sandwich, take the coffee, take whatever it is she thinks I need.

But I don't. I just sit there, back against the cold metal of the bench, watching her, watching the world move around us like we're both stuck in a time loop, a moment that won't end.

She sighs. A soft sound, like she's not sure what to do with me. She places the coffee and sandwich on the ground next to me. Not too close, just within reach, as if she's giving me a choice. Like she's letting me decide whether or not I'm worth her time.

"I don't trust people," I finally say. It's not an apology. It's not an explanation. It's just the truth, raw and ugly. "People don't do shit like this for nothing. You got an agenda. A reason. Everyone's got an agenda."

She looks at me for a long time, eyes searching mine like she's trying to read the fine print of my life. I don't make it easy. No one does. Not here. Not in this city. Not when you've been kicked around and thrown away by people who should have cared, by the people who don't even bother to notice you when you're lying on the ground, bleeding and broken.

"I know," she says, and I can hear something in her voice—maybe sadness, maybe resignation, but there's nothing fake about it. She's not smiling anymore. She's just talking to me. And in a strange way, it feels like she's talking to the part of me that's still human. "I know it's hard to trust. I know people can be cruel. But... I'm not trying to fix you. I'm not trying to save you. I'm just trying to do something small. Just this."

I stare at her, not knowing what to say. Not knowing how to let someone in again. It's been years since anyone's talked to me like that—like they're not afraid of me, like they don't see me as less than human, like I'm not just another broken thing to toss aside. I don't know what to make of it.

She bends down slowly, just in case I try to pull away, and her fingers brush the edge of the sandwich. It's nothing—just a little gesture, but for some reason, it hits me like a truck.

"You don't have to trust me," she says softly, her voice not forceful but steady. "Just take the coffee. Take the food. Take what I can give. And if you don't want it, I'll walk away. No strings attached."

There's no irony in her words. No hidden agenda. No game. Just the offer of something simple, something real. And for the first time in a long time, I wonder if I'm the one who's been wrong all this time. I wonder if I've built so many walls around myself that I've forgotten what it feels like to be treated like a person. Just a person.

I don't take the sandwich. Not yet. But I reach for the coffee. And for the first time in years, I drink something that wasn't stolen or forced on me by someone who thought I was worthless.

And for a moment, I think maybe the world isn't as dark as I thought it was. Maybe.

A Brief Conversation

The coffee's bitter, scalding my throat like the world's trying to teach me a lesson I'll never learn. I take another sip, not for the taste, but for the momentary distraction. My hands shake a little—not from the cold but from something deeper, something that stirs inside of me when I look at her.

She stands there, holding out a half-wrapped sandwich, a disposable cup of coffee in the other hand, and her eyes—there's something in those eyes that makes my insides churn. Not pity. Not sympathy. No, it's something worse. Something worse than that cold stare the world always gives me. It's the kind of gaze that makes you feel like you've been caught, even if you don't know what crime you're guilty of.

She must have seen something in me when she walked by. She must have thought I looked like someone worth saving, worth helping. They all think that. The ones who want to do good, the ones who need to feel like they've done something worthwhile. I've had them all. The do-gooders, the saviors, the angels. The ones who hand you a couple of bucks or a sandwich like it's going to make you forget that you're nothing but a stain on the sidewalk to them.

Her voice cuts through the air, quiet but firm, "If you want to talk... I'm here."

There's a softness in her tone that makes me want to crawl out of my own skin. I swallow hard, feel the bitterness of the coffee again, but it's not enough to burn away the feeling that's spreading inside me—something warm and sickly, something I don't want to feel. I don't need to talk. I don't need anything from her, especially not pity.

I look at her for a long time, weighing her like she's some kind of puzzle I can't solve. Her hair is dark, falling loose around her face. She's got that look—the one that says she means well, but doesn't have a clue.

I take a long drag from the coffee, just to give myself a reason not to say anything. My fingers are cold around the paper cup, but my body's starting to burn with something—something I don't want to name. The last thing I need is a connection.

"I don't need to talk." The words are like rocks falling from my mouth, rough, harsh. I don't trust her enough to let her hear the things that are lodged in my chest. There's no room in me for kindness, not anymore. Not after everything that's been done to me, by the world, by people who pretended to care.

She just nods, like she's not surprised. Like she's heard it before. I bet she has. They all think they can fix it, fix me. But they never do. They never get close enough.

She shifts her weight, like she's testing the ground between us. I'm not sure if she's going to press me, ask again. I don't give her the satisfaction of waiting.

"Shelters," I spit the word like it's poison. "They don't do shit. You feed 'em, give 'em a bed for the night, then you kick 'em back to the streets to get chewed up again. All this so-called 'help'—it's a fucking joke."

I can hear the bitterness in my voice, the edge that I try to keep hidden. But it slips out anyway. Every word feels like a confession, like I'm not just rejecting her offer of help, but the world that comes with it. I hear myself, and I can't stop the disgust that churns in my gut.

Marie doesn't flinch. She doesn't back away. She just stands there, watching me with those eyes—eyes that seem to see more than I want them to.

"I know it's not perfect," she says softly, almost like she's speaking to herself more than to me. "But it's something. Better than nothing."

She's not wrong. I know that. I've been in those shelters, the ones where you get fed and bedded down like an animal at the pound. But it's never enough. Never enough to make a man feel like he's human again. You wake up every day to the same mess, the same fucked-up world, and it never changes. It's just more of the same. More of the nothing that's already gnawing away at you.

I'm tired. I'm so fucking tired of hearing this. I'm tired of people trying to fix me, trying to fix this mess. I don't need to be saved. The truth is, I've given up on salvation a long time ago.

But there's something in her voice, something in the way she holds herself, that makes me want to say more. Makes me want to show her what's under the layers. The filth, the scars, the things I hide so deep inside that not even I want to face them. But I won't. I can't. Because if I let her in, if I let anyone in, they'll just leave.

I take a breath, trying to settle the storm in my chest. I turn my face away, not because I'm ashamed, but because I'm tired of pretending. Tired of holding up the walls between us.

"I don't need saving," I say, quieter this time.

She looks at me like she knows I'm lying. She doesn't argue. Doesn't offer me anything else. She just watches, her eyes calm, steady, like she's waiting for something—maybe for me to break. Maybe for me to finally say the things I'm too afraid to say.

The silence stretches on between us, thick and uncomfortable. It feels like I've got a thousand things left unsaid, a million cracks I don't want her to see. And maybe she's waiting for me to speak them.

But I don't. I won't.

She looks down at the sandwich again, then back at me. It's that look again—the flicker of disappointment, not in me, but in the world. It's like she's starting to understand something. Something I wish I didn't have to show her.

Finally, she nods, a soft, almost sad smile tugging at her lips. "Take care of yourself," she says.

It's the last thing she says before she turns and walks away, her footsteps disappearing into the noise of the city. I watch her go, my heart a stone in my chest. I don't know why I can't move. Can't bring myself to call after her, to ask her to stay. It's like I'm frozen in place, stuck in this moment, as if all the years of rejection, of being used, of choosing to be alone have led me to this.

This brief, useless connection.

I sit there for a while, the coffee long gone cold. The sandwich untouched. I think about getting up, moving on, but the weight of her words, the faint trace of something like understanding, hangs heavy. It's easier to stay in the dark, easier to keep pretending nothing matters.

But it doesn't feel the same anymore. Not with her gone. And I don't know what to do with that.

The Seed of Hope

I watch her leave, her footsteps soft but certain, each one echoing a reminder of something I'd rather not feel. Marie. That name sticks in my throat like a knot, tight and unfamiliar. I can't remember the last time someone cared enough to give a damn. Maybe that's what makes her different. She doesn't want anything from me. At least, I don't think she does.

Her voice still lingers in my head, like a song I can't quite remember but know was good once. I see the city swallowing her up, turning her into just another stranger in a crowd of ghosts. She's got a life, I'm sure of it. Some warm apartment, or a job that makes her feel like she's going somewhere. Maybe a boyfriend, maybe even a fucking dog to walk in the morning, while I—while I... wait. What the hell do I do? I don't even remember what it's like to not wait for the next shitstorm.

I reach for the coffee, the one she left behind. It's still warm, but it's not hers anymore. The heat feels like it's coming from the outside, a brief kind of warmth that's already starting to evaporate. I take a sip, feel it slide down my throat like something medicinal. It's black, too strong. But that's how I take it—too strong, too bitter, just like everything else in this world. The taste lingers, like the memory of something soft that was never mine to keep.

I don't know what she saw in me. What made her stop and offer the fucking sandwich. I try to shrug it off, but there's a pit in my stomach now. A small ache I haven't felt in god knows how long. It's that stupid feeling of wanting something more, like I've been starved of humanity for too long and just that one brief, awkward moment of connection—just a smile, a hand outstretched—was enough to make me feel like I was maybe, just maybe, worth a second glance.

It's pathetic, isn't it? Thinking that maybe this—her little kindness—could change anything. But you know how it goes. People come. People go. And the world keeps turning. Nothing ever sticks.

I've been on this street too long, watching the parade of lives pass me by. How many times have I seen someone like her before? The white knight syndrome. The goddamn savior complex that's supposed to make me feel better about myself, but just makes me feel smaller. A temporary distraction. That's all I am. A stopgap. A broken thing to be fixed, for a moment, before they move on to their next task. Another homeless face, another sad story they can drop in a charity box and forget about.

But I'm not one to take the pity. No, I don't want that. I never wanted it. I'd rather drown in this cesspool than let anyone feel sorry for me. You think I'm weak? I'm not. I'm surviving, and that's more than I can say for a lot of these bastards walking around with their fancy lives. At least I don't have to pretend. At least I'm honest.

I feel that familiar bitterness bubbling up. It's a gut punch, a cocktail of anger and shame. It's been my constant companion. When she offered the coffee, I could've turned it away. But I didn't. She didn't know what I really needed. She thought I needed food, but I don't. Food won't fix me. Nothing will. I can already taste the futility on the back of my tongue.

"Do you want to talk?" she asked me, as if I could ever say yes to that. I looked at her, seeing the kindness in her eyes, and I wanted to laugh. People like her don't get it. They think a conversation can change everything. That it's just a matter of telling the right words, sharing the right space. But I've been talking for years, and nobody listens. I used to talk to myself, but I didn't even listen then.

But I didn't say any of that. I just shook my head, gave her some bullshit about not needing help, because that's all I ever do. Push people away. Like I'm some kind of goddamn fortress. A fortress made of broken bottles and empty promises. If she knew anything, she'd leave me the hell alone.

Still, something in her eyes—the way she looked at me, like she could see right through the mess I've become—it rattles me. I try to shake it off. Keep it buried. But it's there now. That soft ache. That flicker of hope that burns out faster than a match.

I can feel it—the seed, so goddamn small, so fragile, I want to crush it before it grows any bigger. But there it is, buried deep in my chest, lodged between my ribs. Hope. Stupid, idiotic hope. I know what happens when you let that shit in. You get attached. You start to care. And then the world comes along and kicks you in the teeth.

She's gone now. Vanished into the city's guts. It's the same city that swallowed me whole years ago and never let me back up for air. I take another sip of the coffee, but it tastes like ash now. I toss it aside and watch it spill, mixing with the grime that already coats the pavement.

A HAPPY DEATH

I want to scream, want to shout at the sky, at the city, at everyone who's never looked at me like I matter. But that would be a waste of breath. I've screamed too many times and the only thing I've gotten is the echo of my own voice, bouncing off buildings that don't care, people that don't care.

So I sit here, alone, and I let the ache in my chest grow. Because it's easier to feel something, anything, than to let it die. Because part of me doesn't want to let it die. Part of me wants to believe she was real. That maybe, just maybe, there's something left worth fighting for.

But the city doesn't care about that. Neither does she.

I can already feel the walls closing in again. The bitter, suffocating walls of self-doubt, of shame, of everything I've ever been. And I won't let her memory stay long. I won't let it.

I'll bury it like all the other things that never mattered, like all the other people who've come and gone. But for now, I let it sit there. Just for a second. A stupid, fucking second.

Maybe tomorrow I'll try again. Or maybe I won't.

But right now, the only thing I know for sure is that I'm still here.

And that, somehow, is enough.

Chapter 4: Frank's Arrival

The Old Survivor

I'd seen him before, but today he was different. Frank wasn't just another bum off the street, a ghost slinking through the cracks in New York. No, Frank was a monument—damaged, fractured, but still standing, still breathing. His face was a topography of pain, an atlas of the years spent weathering a world that didn't care. Every wrinkle on his skin was a battlefield. Every scar told a story. He looked like a man who had been kicked down so many times he'd stopped noticing the bruises.

Frank didn't ease into the space beside me like someone unsure of their place. He just planted himself there, heavy and solid, like he was staking his claim. The smell hit me first—a toxic mix of old sweat, liquor, tobacco, and something far worse, something that lingered even after he spoke. "You look like shit," he rasped, his voice thick like tar, roughened by years of whiskey and smoke.

I didn't even look at him. He was right. I did look like shit. My skin felt loose, stretched tight over a frame that had stopped caring. Maybe I was just a body going through the motions. Maybe I was already dead.

“Thanks,” I muttered, but it sounded weak, even to me. What could I say? It was true. I hadn't seen a mirror in days, but I could feel it. My eyes sunken, my clothes ragged, my body more a carcass than anything human.

Frank just exhaled, the smoke curling around us like a sick fog. His eyes didn't look at me; they didn't need to. He was used to broken people. “You out here living or just existing?” he asked, his voice cutting through the noise like a razor.

I didn't know how to answer. Was I alive? Was I? I was more a shadow of someone who once was than anything resembling a person. But Frank wasn't asking for an answer. He wasn't giving a damn.

"Surviving," I said. But the word tasted like something foul in my mouth. Surviving wasn't living. It was just getting by. And getting by wasn't enough.

Frank's lips curled into a grimace. "Surviving, huh?" He let the word hang in the air like a dirty rag. "You ain't surviving, kid. You're just waitin' for somethin' to kill you."

The words stabbed me straight in the gut. I wanted to lash out, to tell him he didn't know me. But he did know me. Hell, he knew me better than I knew myself. I wasn't surviving. I wasn't even trying. I was just... here. Another anonymous soul waiting for the end.

Frank flicked his cigarette, watching the ember fade out, like it was something more important than it was. "You think any of these assholes are gonna save you?" he said, nodding toward the herd of people huddled outside the soup kitchen, their faces blank, their eyes vacant. "You think they'll toss you a dollar or a smile because you look hungry? Nah. They're not lookin' at you. You're a problem to be dealt with, a piece of garbage they don't wanna see. They'll drop a coin in your cup, sure. But that's it. You think they care? They don't."

I didn't argue. I didn't have the energy for it. It wasn't just the people at the soup kitchen who didn't care. Nobody cared. Not the cops, not the corporations, not the politicians with their thousand-dollar suits and fake smiles. The world was built to chew you up and spit you out, and nobody was coming to stop it.

"You know what those people see when they look at you?" Frank asked, his voice barely above a growl. "They see what they don't want to be. And then they keep walking." He leaned forward, eyes narrow, like he was about to say something that would change my life. "You wanna eat?" he said, his voice thick with disgust. "You don't ask. You don't beg. You take."

I blinked. It took a moment for the words to register. Take? What did he mean? Steal? Rob someone?

"Yeah," Frank continued, leaning in closer, his breath hot against my face. "You walk up to that hot dog stand, grab what you need, and you don't blink. You think they're gonna chase you? They'll get mad, sure. Maybe they'll shout.

Maybe they'll call the cops. Maybe. But you don't look back. You just take it. You know why? 'Cause they don't give a damn about you, or anybody else."

I felt a chill run through me. It was wrong. It was desperate. It was everything I'd been taught to avoid. But at the same time, it felt like the only thing that made sense. I'd spent my whole life trying to survive with the scraps they gave me—begging, hoping for a handout, waiting for someone to give a shit.

Frank leaned back, watching me, watching my eyes, waiting for something to click. "That's how it is out here. You ain't no charity case. You ain't no cause. You're just a piece of meat in a world that don't care about your problems. You take what you need, and you keep moving. Don't apologize for it. You think they're gonna give you a seat at their table? Fuck that. You don't even get a seat. The world's a game, and if you wanna stay in it, you play by its rules. And the rules are: Take. Take everything you can."

I wanted to argue. I wanted to tell him there had to be more to life than this. But when I opened my mouth, the words didn't come. It was like something inside me had died a long time ago, and now, I was just going through the motions. Frank wasn't asking me to believe in anything. He wasn't asking me to change. He was just telling me how to survive.

"Everything's a hustle out here," Frank went on. "The street don't care about who you were or who you could have been. It's all about what you can take. Take what's yours, and don't feel bad about it. Nobody else will." He cracked his neck, a sound like bones snapping, and stood up, slow and deliberate, like he had all the time in the world.

"You got tomorrow," he muttered, his voice a low growl. "But you better be ready. 'Cause tomorrow ain't gonna be any better than today if you keep waiting for somebody to save you."

And with that, he walked off, vanishing into the crowd like he was nothing, like he'd never existed. But his words—those words—stuck to me. They clung to my skin, gnawed at me like rats in the dark.

I stayed where I was for a while, letting his words echo through my head, like a song I couldn't stop playing. Take. Take. Take.

It wasn't just about food. It was about everything. Everything that the world had stolen from me, everything I'd been too scared to claim. Frank was right. The world didn't owe me a goddamn thing.

Tomorrow, I thought. Tomorrow, I'd take what was mine. Tomorrow, I would stop asking for scraps. I would stop waiting. I would take.

The city buzzed around me, alive with noise, alive with everything that I wasn't. But tomorrow, maybe I'd start living. Maybe I'd start taking.

The Morality of Survival

I woke up face down on the pavement, the city still spinning from the night before, and the cold concrete biting through the thin fabric of my jacket like it knew I had nowhere else to be. The air had that sour tang of piss and cheap booze, the odor of life lived outside, exposed to everything. I pushed myself up, not out of pride, but because there was nowhere else to go. Frank was gone. I didn't expect him to stay.

I didn't know what I expected anymore.

The hunger gnawed at me, but it wasn't food I was missing. It was more like something essential—something I couldn't name, something that had slipped away piece by piece, and I hadn't even noticed. I dragged myself off the curb and tried to make myself look halfway decent, like some kind of normal human being, though I knew better. There were no mirrors on these streets. You didn't get to see yourself until you were too far gone to do anything about it.

I found Frank leaning against a lamppost by the corner, a half-smoked cigarette dangling from his lip. He looked like he belonged there—like he was born to roam these streets. The way he carried himself, like the world owed him nothing, made me wonder how much of that was learned and how much of it was just instinct. Maybe it was a little of both.

I shoved my hands in my pockets, trying to look casual, but he saw right through it. "Still think you can survive on your moral high ground?" Frank asked, his voice rough from years of smoke and hard living. He eyed me like he could smell the softness in me, like I was the last piece of meat on the bone.

I didn't respond. There was nothing to say. Frank already knew the answer.

"You're gonna freeze out here, kid. You're gonna starve." He took another drag from his cigarette, letting the smoke curl into the gray morning air. "And you'll die. Maybe not today, but soon enough. You wanna know how to survive out here? You wanna know what keeps you breathing when everyone else falls off? It ain't kindness. It ain't compassion. It's raw, ugly self-preservation. Survival."

I hated that he was right, but he was. The truth always hurt, especially when it was too real to ignore.

I turned away, watching the traffic buzz by, trying to focus on anything but Frank's words. But I couldn't. It was like trying to shut out the sound of a train barreling down the tracks, deafening and inevitable.

"Look," Frank said, pushing off the lamppost and taking a step toward me. "You still got a lot of fantasy in you. You think you can live like some saint. But out here? Ain't no saints. Ain't no heroes. There's just you and what you'll do to stay alive. You want food? You gotta steal. You want a place to sleep? You gotta take it. You can't sit around waiting for someone to hand it to you."

I felt a sting in my chest, like his words were razor blades, cutting through whatever naive part of me still thought I could be different. The idea that I could be anything other than what the streets made me seemed so far away now. I didn't want to hear it, but it was there—his voice, the weight of it settling in, planting seeds of doubt in my mind. And it was too late to pull them out.

"I'm not like you," I muttered, but the words felt weak, like they weren't my own. Frank grinned, the same grin he always wore—like a man who'd seen it all and found it all to be a joke.

"You don't get it, do you? You think you can still be the man you were before? You think you can walk around this city like some damn good Samaritan, trying to be kind to every hungry face you see? Ain't no room for that here." His voice softened, just enough for me to hear the truth in it. "You ain't gonna make it if you don't get your hands dirty."

I looked down, my hands buried deep in the pockets of my jacket. What was left of me? What was left to even fight for? Was I just some corpse already, trying to pretend I was alive? The realization hit me like a ton of bricks—Frank wasn't just talking about survival. He was talking about something darker. Something deeper.

"Then what do I do?" I asked, the question coming out before I could stop it.

Frank paused, like he was considering whether to lie or tell me the truth. The truth was always worse, but it was the only thing that would stick.

"You do what you gotta do," he said, his eyes narrowing as if he was looking right through me. "You adapt. You kill the softness inside you. You stop caring about who's starving, who's freezing, who's dying. You don't have time for that. You got your own problems."

It was like he'd taken a hammer to my chest and cracked open everything that used to matter. Everything I thought I could hang onto. I wanted to argue, to scream at him that he was wrong. But I knew, deep down, that I didn't have the strength anymore. I didn't even have the will.

Frank was right. The streets didn't care about your soul, or your moral code, or how much you cared about the people you passed by. They only cared about whether you were strong enough to stand up and face the next day. Or whether you were weak enough to let it crush you.

He dropped his cigarette, grinding it under his heel, and turned to leave, the echo of his footsteps sharp in the silence. "The only rule out here is the one you make for yourself," he called over his shoulder. "You keep pretending there's another way, and the world's gonna eat you alive."

I stood there, frozen, staring after him. The city moved around me, oblivious, like it always did. People walked past, heads down, wrapped in their own lives, and I wondered how many of them were like me—too afraid to admit the truth about the world we lived in. Too afraid to see what we'd become.

But Frank had already given me the answer. Survival was the only truth that mattered. The rest was just noise.

And that was it. That was all there was.

The Seduction of Cynicism

I hate how the city looks at night. It's got that look, the kind that's as fake as a smile on a politician. The lights are just drowning out the truth—the dark truth I'm starting to accept. It's not about hope. It's not about some better tomorrow. It's about today, right now. And I hate it more and more because I'm starting to understand Frank's version of it. I'm starting to see the world the way he does.

You get used to the sounds—the hum of the machines, the sirens, the groan of the subway echoing through the streets. People keep their heads down, like they're too scared to look up, scared of seeing the truth in someone else's eyes, because the truth's ugly. It's the kind of ugly you can't scrub off with soap or tears. But here's the trick: if you stop pretending, it stops hurting. Frank says it all the time: "Stop giving a shit. You can't survive if you're still trying to be decent. That shit'll get you killed faster than the cold or the rats."

I'm starting to believe him.

I watch Frank as he works his angles. He's an artist of the streets. Doesn't even have to try. He's got this face, like a man who's seen everything, and nothing shocks him anymore. A jaded bastard in a stained overcoat, his eyes burning through the crap people toss his way, sizing up their souls like a butcher sizing up meat. He's not a beggar, he's a predator. And for the first time in my life, I feel the heat of that kind of hunger. Not the kind for food, but the kind for survival. The kind that tells you to cut everyone else down before they get a chance to do it to you.

I'm starting to hate myself for it.

"You know what the trick is, Dez?" Frank asks one night, his voice low and smooth, like he's sharing the secret to life. "It's not about being kind. Kindness is a weakness. It's about being useful. You make yourself useful to the right people, you get what you need."

"Useful?" I ask. I know what he means, but I want him to say it. I want to hear it from his mouth.

"Yeah. You make yourself indispensable. A helping hand. A quick joke. A shoulder to lean on when they're drunk enough to trust you. It's not about compassion, kid. It's about control. And control gives you the power to take what you want, when you want."

I feel a cold knot in my stomach. Something sharp and twisted. I don't want to admit that the words taste a little too familiar now. Frank's got me thinking about things I used to shut out—how kindness is a goddamn joke when you're starving, how morality's just a luxury for those who don't need to fight for scraps.

Frank's been schooling me in survival tactics—small cons, tricks, stealing from the right people at the right time, making myself seem helpless enough that no one sees the thief in me. It's dirty. It's ugly. But damn, it works. You wouldn't believe how easy it is to play the fool.

It's hard to say what feels worse—the acts themselves, or the way I don't even think twice anymore. When Frank makes his moves, there's no hesitation. He'll lift a wallet out of someone's coat pocket like it's nothing, slipping it into his sleeve with the grace of a magician. "You do it right," he says, "you never get caught."

It's easy to think it's all bullshit, until you realize you've started doing the same damn thing. I watch myself in the reflection of a store window one night—dirty hair, an old jacket that smells like piss and cheap booze, eyes a little too wild. I don't recognize the man looking back at me. Hell, I don't know who I'm becoming.

I tell myself it's just a phase. That I'm just playing the game to survive. But the game is starting to seep into my blood, and I don't know how much longer I can convince myself I'm still the same person.

The truth is, I've stopped thinking about the people I used to care about. My family, the ones I abandoned long ago because it was easier to leave than to let them see what I'd become. I used to think about them when I was alone, lying on the concrete, freezing my ass off. But now, now I only think about surviving. About getting through the next minute, the next hour. If that means throwing a punch or taking what's not mine, then so be it.

I tell myself I'm not Frank. I'm not the same as him, right? I still have something left. But I can feel it, that slippery slope. Every time I close my eyes and listen to Frank spin his tales, I feel that part of me—my soul, or whatever's left of it—slipping away. I can't deny it anymore. Frank is both the man I admire and the man I fear. He's everything I could become if I'm not careful. He's a mentor, a model, and a cautionary tale all rolled into one.

It's not just the survival tactics he teaches me, it's the philosophy behind them. There's no room for idealism on the streets, he says. "You think the world gives a shit? It doesn't. It never did. You're just a cog in the machine. The only way to stay alive is to work the machine to your advantage. Otherwise, it grinds you up, and you'll never even know it."

I want to resist. I want to believe there's something more, something better than this. But the streets are wearing me down, and Frank's logic is starting to make too much sense.

I watch him with a mix of awe and horror, because I'm starting to see the man who's lived through it all, and the man who's forgotten everything worth holding onto. Frank's eyes are as cold as steel, and I can feel the chill creeping into my bones. I'm starting to see through the mask, the one I thought was real.

I don't want to end up like Frank. But I'm starting to wonder if I already have.

Chapter 5: Officer Johnson

The Law and the Street

It's early enough that most of them are still asleep—those who think they matter. The suits, the skirts, walking like they own the goddamn world. Heads held high. Eyes locked on their screens, too busy to see anything real. Too busy to see me.

But that's fine. I don't need their eyes. I've gotten used to being invisible.

The air smells like burnt coffee, exhaust, and sweat. The kind of sweat that never dries off. But that's nothing. The real smell is the one that sticks to you, the one you can't scrub away. The smell of being forgotten. The smell of not mattering. It's the stench of a thousand bodies the world stepped over, left to rot on its own sidewalk.

I rub my eyes, but it's no use. There's no escaping the noise. Car horns, sirens, people shouting, cursing, like any of it means anything. It all bleeds together now. A buzzing in my head, like a fly too stupid to know it's already dead. The city never sleeps. And neither do I.

Then I see him.

And every day it's the same story.

Officer Johnson. He walks like he's wearing the world as a crown. His neck's too thick, his jaw too square. He thinks his badge makes him something more than human, like it's a goddamn shield. He patrols this street like it's his own little kingdom, the rest of us just parasites feeding off his charity. He looks down on me like I'm dirt. And he's right—I am. But I'm not the kind of dirt you scrape off your shoes.

He sees me. I see him.

His eyes narrow, and the words come, like they always do. "Move along, or I'll give you a ticket."

I flick the cigarette onto the ground, watching the ember die out. The defiance rises in me. It's always there, like a sick joke. I don't move.

"You've got no business here," he says, flat voice, no conviction, just a line he's memorized. "Get up. Move along."

I don't flinch. I don't even blink.

"Or what?" I say, voice rough like gravel grinding against steel. "You gonna arrest me for sitting here? Maybe toss me in a cage with the rest of the animals you think we are?"

His boots thud against the pavement, too loud, too deliberate. He's getting closer, stepping into my space like he's got the right to control it. But he doesn't. He never did. Not in my world.

His shadow falls over me. I don't shrink from it. I've been pushed down too many times to give a damn. Too many men like him—shiny shoes, shiny badges—looking down like I'm less than dirt, less than nothing. They want to break me. They want to crush me beneath their feet. But I'm still here. And I won't move.

"I'll give you one chance," he growls, voice like nails on a chalkboard. "Move, or I'll write you up. You'll go to jail. You'll get a record. That's gonna be worse for you."

His words hang in the air like a dead fly. A ticket? A record? Like it'll change anything. Like it matters.

I look up at him. "You think a piece of paper means anything to me? You think you can scare me with your badge? You don't own this street. You don't own me. You don't even know me."

His jaw clenches, eyes flashing, like he's trying to hold back the rage. But it's not about rage. It's about power. The kind he thinks he has. The kind he's never going to get from me.

He's not in charge here. He never was. He's just a cog in the machine. A soldier in a war he doesn't understand. A part of the system that grinds people like me into dust, then throws us away like we don't matter.

I can see it in his eyes now—he knows I'm right. But he'll never admit it. He can't. Because admitting it would mean admitting he's just another pawn. Just another player in a game he can't win.

His hand hovers near his belt, and for a second, I think he'll pull out a baton or cuffs, maybe remind me that violence is his only answer. But I'm not scared of that. I've seen it all before.

"I don't have time for this," he mutters, turning away. He thinks he's won, that I'll just slink back into the shadows.

But I don't move. I don't have anywhere to go.

I watch him walk away, his boots thumping against the pavement like a heartbeat I can't escape. I wonder if he ever thinks about the people he's crushing under his boots. Does he wonder why we're here? Does he ever ask himself why we're so broken? Does he know this street doesn't belong to him? It doesn't belong to anyone. Not really.

Maybe I'll never leave. Maybe this is it for me. But I'm not begging for scraps from a system that's already decided I don't matter.

"Yeah," I mutter, taking another drag from my cigarette. "You'll be back, Officer Johnson. You'll always come back."

But I'll still be here. Waiting.

The Power Play

The city doesn't sleep, but sometimes I wish it would. It keeps moving, always moving, like it's trying to outrun something it's too scared to face. The concrete and glass, the cold, heartless structures—these things never stop. It's the people who make the noise. The cars honk, the sirens wail in the distance, the footsteps tap-tap-tap across the sidewalk like someone's counting down to something. But it's never my time. Not yet. Not for me.

I've been here long enough to understand how it works. I don't need to look at the clock to know when the suits start flooding the streets. They've got their noses buried in their phones, their hands clutching their overpriced coffee cups, pretending the world isn't falling apart around them. They don't see me. They never see me. I'm just another stain on the pavement, another ghost they've learned to step over.

I'm used to it. Used to being invisible.

And every day it's the same story. Maybe I shouldn't have slept in the same place 2 days in a row?

I see Johnson before he sees me, just the way I see every cop coming. It's not hard. You learn to recognize the sound of boots scraping against the sidewalk, the familiar creak of a leather belt, the soft hiss of a radio somewhere on their hip. But Johnson's not just any cop. He's got a swagger in his step, like he owns the sidewalk. The way his shoulders are squared, his jaw set like he's on a mission. I've seen guys like him before. The ones who think a badge gives them the right to look down on everyone else. The ones who wear their authority like armor, as if it makes them better, as if they're somehow above the people they're supposed to serve.

He doesn't look at me like I'm human. He looks at me like I'm a problem. A rat in a corner that needs to be flushed out.

And that's the thing—I'm not just a nuisance to him. I'm a reminder. A reminder of everything he thinks he's better than. A reminder that people like me are always on the fringes, always waiting for the next boot to come down on us, to remind us where we belong.

But I'm not going anywhere.

He stops in front of me, blocking the little bit of sunlight I had left. His shadow falls over me like a weight, like he's trying to crush the air out of my lungs. I flick my cigarette onto the ground, watching the ember die. It's all just a game to him. I know how this goes. He's been doing this long enough. He'll try to intimidate me, throw his weight around. He'll talk like he's got all the power, like he can make me do whatever he wants.

But I'm done with that.

"Move along," he says. His voice is cold, all authority, no warmth. It's the same words he's said a hundred times before. The same script he's memorized like he's playing some part in a show.

And I know my script, too.

I don't move. I just look up at him, my eyes steady. I can feel his gaze on me, judging me, weighing me. He's waiting for me to break, to flinch, to get up and do what he says. But I won't. I've been here too long. I've been pushed around too many times to let him get the satisfaction.

"You got something else to say?" I ask, my voice rough, gravel grinding against metal. "You gonna give me a ticket? Maybe drag me off to jail? You think that's gonna scare me? Make me bend to your will?"

I see his jaw tighten. He's been trained for this, I can tell. He knows the rules. He knows how this game is supposed to go. But I'm not playing by them.

He leans in a little closer, the stench of his cologne cutting through the stale air between us. I can smell the cheap soap on his skin, the leather of his belt. He thinks he can break me with a few words, but he doesn't understand. He doesn't understand what it feels like to live like this. To know that you're not even seen as a person anymore, just a problem to be solved. He doesn't understand what it means to wake up every day and feel like the world is doing everything it can to push you into the dirt.

He steps closer, his boots thudding against the sidewalk. I feel the heat coming off his body, his shadow swallowing mine. He's too close now. I can almost feel his anger, bubbling just under the surface. But it doesn't matter.

"Move," he says again, like it's a command, like it's the only word he knows. "Or I'll have to arrest you."

I look up at him, my eyes narrowing. The anger wells up in me, but it's not the same kind of anger he's expecting. I'm not scared of him. I'm not scared of his baton or his handcuffs or whatever bullshit threat he's got ready. The only thing I'm scared of is being invisible forever. The only thing I'm scared of is the system he's part of—the system that's got its foot on my neck, pushing me down, telling me I don't matter.

"You think a ticket's gonna fix anything?" I say, my voice rising now, stronger than it's been in a long time. "You think you can erase me with a piece of paper? You think you're better than me just because you wear that badge? You're nothing but a cog in the machine. And you don't even know it."

I can see it in his eyes then. That flicker of doubt. That tiny moment where he realizes I'm right. He's not the law. He's just another guy doing a job. But that job has made him believe he's something more. He's bought into the lie. And now he's stuck in it, just like everyone else.

For a moment, he doesn't say anything. He just stands there, looking at me like he's trying to figure me out. His jaw's clenched, his fists are tight at his sides. I can see the rage building inside him, but it's not the same kind of rage that's building inside me. His is the rage of someone who's been trained to see things in black and white. Mine is the rage of someone who knows there's nothing but gray, and that gray is a slow death.

"I don't have time for this," he mutters, like he's disgusted. Like I'm a waste of his time.

And that's when it hits me. He doesn't care about the law. He doesn't care about justice. He cares about power. He cares about making sure I know my place in the world. He cares about crushing people like me, keeping us down so the ones at the top can keep their grip on everything.

I don't move. I don't give him the satisfaction.

And as he walks away, I sit there for a moment longer, letting the city swallow me whole. He'll be back. They always come back. But I'll still be here, waiting. And maybe that's the only power I've got left.

Maybe that's all any of us have.

A Moment of Humanity

I've seen that look before. The one Officer Johnson gives me, a mix of disdain and indifference.

For three days I've slept in the same place. I shouldn't do that. I forgot.

But today it's different. His eyes don't burn with contempt. They don't flicker with the glee of power. Today, they look through me, like I'm not even there. Like I'm just another smear on the sidewalk, fading into the cracks. It's the kind of look that makes you realize: You don't matter. Not to him. Not to the system. Not to anyone.

I should've felt relief. I should've felt like I was winning some kind of invisible victory over him, but I didn't. The realization hit me harder than any slap in the face. It's not hatred, not disgust, not even pity. He doesn't care about me at all. I'm just a speck, a momentary nuisance to him, a fly buzzing around the rim of his coffee cup. And then I'm gone. Gone from his thoughts, gone from his world. I'm nothing. No one.

And that's worse than hate.

The indifference was suffocating. I could feel it clogging up my lungs, like the city air, thick with smoke and exhaust, seeping into my bones. The weight of it crushed me—suddenly, completely. The police aren't just an obstacle to people like me; they're the ones who make sure we stay invisible. Their job isn't just to enforce the law, it's to erase people like me, without a second thought. To make sure that the machinery of this city keeps churning, grinding down everything in its path, while I just fade into the background. To disappear.

I was just some bum sitting on the street, taking up space, a shadow in a city of too many shadows. He was a cog in the machine. And so was I. We both just played our parts. I was just unlucky enough to be the part they throw away.

That's the game. You get one shot. You take what you can and hope no one notices when you fall out of the frame.

He looks at me again, but this time there's no challenge in his eyes. No anger, no authority. He's just... done. And so am I.

"You're not gonna make a scene, are you?" he asks, his voice flat, almost bored. Like I'm some problem he'd rather forget about than deal with.

I take a drag off my cigarette. The ember burns bright for a second, then dies. I don't say anything. I don't need to. I'm not here to fight him. Not anymore.

The silence hangs there between us like something thick and sticky, too heavy to escape. And I feel the rage, the hollow ache, creep back in. The kind of rage that never really goes away. It's like a wound that never heals, no matter how much you try to ignore it. The rage of knowing that you don't matter to anyone. To the cops. To the suits that walk by, heads down, eyes glued to their phones. To the people who keep walking without a glance, as if I'm not even here. And the thing is, they're right. I'm not here. Not to them.

"Move along, or I'll call it in," he says, and I can hear the emptiness in his voice. I hear the repetition in his words. They're the same lines he's said a thousand times before. The same lines he'll say a thousand more. The city has rules. The city has orders. And I am just one more person who doesn't fit in them.

I flick the cigarette, feeling the weight of it disappear. It's nothing, just a little spark in the dark. It doesn't matter. Nothing matters anymore. Not his threats. Not his uniform. Not the badge on his chest or the boots on his feet. They're all just parts of a system that doesn't care if I live or die. They don't care if I stand up or stay down. They just want me to move, to disappear.

"Go ahead," I say. "Call it in. I've got nothing left to lose. You can arrest me, fine. You can throw me in a cell and forget about me like everyone else does. But nothing changes. Nothing ever changes. Not for me. Not for anyone."

His face tightens. There's something there, something flickering just behind his eyes. I see it. Maybe it's guilt. Maybe it's doubt. Maybe it's just the realization that I'm right. And he doesn't want to admit it. But he's not going to do anything. He's not going to arrest me. He's not going to help me. He's just going to keep walking. Because that's his job. To keep moving. To keep everything running smoothly, even if it means kicking people like me to the curb.

His hand hovers near his belt for a moment. I brace for it. The baton. The cuffs. I know it's coming. But then he pulls back. His shoulders slump, and his eyes look past me. He doesn't see me. Not really.

"I don't have time for this," he mutters under his breath, turning away.

And I watch him walk off, his boots thudding on the pavement like the beat of a drum. And I think about what he's going to do next. He'll go back to his car. He'll go home. He'll take off his uniform and sit down to a meal, maybe a beer. And maybe, for a second, he'll forget about me. He'll forget about the others like me. He'll forget about the ones who get pushed to the edges, who get stepped on, who get erased.

And I'll be here. Still here. Waiting.

I don't know why I'm still waiting. Maybe I'm not waiting for anything at all. Maybe I'm just waiting for the world to keep turning, for the city to keep grinding, for the next moment to come and go and leave me in the dust like it always does.

But there's a part of me that won't stop. A part of me that keeps holding on to the hope that maybe, just maybe, something might change. Maybe there's a crack in this machine, a way out. Or maybe I'm just too damn tired to care anymore.

But I'll keep breathing, keep waiting, keep standing. Because what else is there?

Chapter 6. Flashback to Ana

Love Lost

I used to love her. I mean, I really loved her. Back then, I wasn't just some pitiful bastard rotting in the corner of this goddamn city, waiting for the world to ignore me. I was a person. I had hope. I had meaning. I had Ana. She made me feel like there was more to life than the miserable parade of half-empty whiskey bottles and crushed cigarettes. We were real together. The world wasn't so big when we were together—just her and me, and a few cracked windows between us.

She had this laugh. A sharp, unfiltered sound that felt like it came from the belly of something bigger than us. It didn't give a shit about all the filth we were stuck in. She didn't care if I was high or drunk, if I smelled like a dumpster or hadn't bathed in three days. She made me feel like I mattered. For a minute, I thought that maybe I did.

The way she looked at me... like I was everything. Like I was worth more than the crack in the street or the crushed cans I used to collect for change. But I couldn't hold on to it. I couldn't hold on to her. My hands were too fucking dirty. Too shaky.

I remember the first time I let her down. It wasn't a big thing. Just a small moment—a promise broken, a lie told, a weight I didn't know how to carry. I'd promised her I wouldn't drink that night. I promised her I'd be better. But I found myself standing in a shitty bar in the middle of nowhere, drowning in some stale vodka that didn't even burn anymore. It just was—and so was I.

When I got home, Ana didn't need to say anything. I could see it in her eyes. The disappointment was a physical thing between us, a knife wound I couldn't stitch up. But she stayed. She stayed because she thought I'd come back. She thought I could fix myself.

And I did try. At first. I went to the meetings, I saw the counselor, I told her things would be different. I wore that same damn mask, the one that looked good from a distance. But up close? It was falling apart. You can't fix a broken man with promises. You can't fix a person who doesn't believe he deserves to be fixed. So, I kept sinking, and Ana kept watching me sink. I could see her getting smaller, like a star in the distance, burning out just a little more every time I reached for another drink.

I remember the last time she left me. The words weren't important anymore. It wasn't a fight. It wasn't a screaming match. She just packed her things, one by one, slow and methodical, like she was doing a favor to herself. No dramatic exit. No slam of the door. She just left.

I watched her walk out of that apartment like she was walking away from a ghost.

And I was a ghost. I didn't feel anything after that. Nothing. No anger. No sadness. I was just numb.

When she was gone, it was like the lights in the world had gone out. The nights felt longer, the days more unbearable. I tried to drown it with whiskey, but I couldn't forget her smile, the way she curled up beside me at night and whispered, "We'll make it through this." The memory cut deeper than any hangover. And still, I tried to push it down, deep into my gut, where it could rot along with the rest of me.

But it didn't work. The pain, the guilt, it stuck to me like tar. And no matter how many bottles I drank, I couldn't wash it off.

I thought I could survive it. But I didn't. I didn't even come close.

There's something strange about love when it's lost. It doesn't feel like the end of the world—not at first. At first, it's just the dull throb of emptiness, like a bruise that's just starting to show. But as the days crawl on, it turns into something heavier. A weight. And you start looking for ways to lighten it. Ways that don't work. Ways that only make it worse.

I could feel her presence everywhere after she was gone. The spaces she used to fill. The kitchen. The bathroom mirror. The bed. I would lay in it for hours, listening to the silence, feeling the void she left behind.

It wasn't just about losing her. It was losing myself. She was the last part of me that still believed in something better, something real. The rest of me was just a shell, a body moving through days I no longer cared about. The addiction wasn't the problem—it was a symptom of a life I didn't know how to live. And without Ana, without her love, I couldn't remember why I wanted to.

I don't even know if I want to anymore.

I see it now, clearer than I ever did before: we were never really a team. Not in the way she needed me to be. I loved her, but I couldn't love her the way she deserved. I couldn't protect her from the storm that I was becoming. The worst part wasn't losing her—it was knowing I never gave her enough of myself to make her stay. She saw the mess I was, but she still thought I could fix myself. Thought that love could fix me.

But you can't love someone back from the dead.

She was the last real thing in my life. And when she walked out that door, she took the only part of me that still had hope. I let her go, and I've been rotting ever since.

I used to think about how I could win her back, how I could clean myself up and stand in front of her, and tell her I was sorry. But I know better now. The truth is, she wouldn't even look at me if I did. There's no going back when you've broken something that bad.

I wasn't enough for Ana. And maybe I wasn't enough for anyone. I thought I had a chance. I thought I could pull myself out of the mess I'd made. But here I am, just a shadow of the man I was when she loved me.

The truth is, I was never the man she thought I was. And that's the thing about love, about life. It all slips away so goddamn fast. One minute you're on top of the world, the next you're buried under it.

And there's no one left to blame but yourself.

The Fall

I was a wreck, that's the truth of it. Nothing more, nothing less. The image of me at that time—a mangled mess of skin and bone, stuffed into a cheap suit—just keeps getting sharper the further I get from it. I should've burned the suit. It was the last damn thing Ana saw me in, and it was the first thing that made her walk out.

I tell myself I didn't care. It's easier that way. Tell yourself something long enough and it becomes the truth. But that's all a lie. I cared. I cared about her laugh, the way her eyes always looked like she could see straight through me, the way I felt like a person when she touched me. But all that was too much for someone like me—too much to handle, too much to keep. It was like holding onto a piece of something good and real, knowing it would slip out of your hands sooner or later.

The days blurred, they always do when you're slipping. One morning, Ana brought me breakfast in bed, smiling like she always did, bringing me toast and coffee with that soft laugh that never failed to make me feel like I could do anything. But those days... they ended. There were no more smiles, no more breakfast, no more anything.

I was lost in the fog, and nothing else mattered but feeding that ache in my gut. I let the woman I loved fade into the distance like an afterthought. She didn't leave me right away. She stood there, watching me turn to dust, waiting for me to snap out of it, waiting for the guy I was when we first met to come back. But he was gone. Dead. Killed by the drink, the needle, the blackness that filled the spaces between my thoughts.

I remember the last time we fought. Her face, flushed with anger, shaking with hurt. It felt like an eternity, the way she looked at me like I wasn't even a person anymore. She wanted me to admit it—that I'd chosen the bottle over her, the high over the life we'd built. But I couldn't. I couldn't admit it because it was true, and the truth was something I couldn't bear. So instead, I lashed out. Not with my fists, but with my words—cheap, ugly, venomous. Words that spat and burned. I told her she was weak. That she couldn't handle me. That I didn't need her to save me.

In the end, she did what I couldn't—she saved herself.

She packed up and left, and I didn't even try to stop her. I stood there, numb, watching her walk out the door, her bags heavy with the remnants of everything we were. I stood there, arms limp at my sides, as the apartment door clicked shut. I told myself that I didn't care. Told myself it was for the best, that I was better off without her—without anyone. But the reality of it sank in later, when the bottles were empty, when the needle didn't numb the pain anymore. Then, I'd try to call her, but my hands would shake so badly I couldn't hold the phone. The number would sit there on the screen, and I'd stare at it until the battery ran out.

I told myself I didn't care. But that was a lie.

The days blurred, and the months stretched out like a bad dream. My body was a stranger, and I didn't recognize the man who stumbled around the streets, dragging a pile of filthy clothes behind him. The woman I loved? She was nothing more than a faint memory now, something that flitted in and out of my head, like a bird caught in a storm. I was sure I'd never hear her laugh again. Sure that the warmth in her eyes, the one that always made me feel like I mattered, would be lost forever. I told myself it didn't matter. I was better off without her.

But that's what addicts do. They lie to themselves because it's easier than facing the truth. Easier than accepting the fact that they destroyed everything.

Ana was my last chance, and I threw her away. I told myself she was the one who couldn't deal with my darkness, but it was me. I was the one who'd built that darkness brick by brick, every lie, every hit, every drink, until the walls were so thick that not even love could tear them down. I thought she could save me. I thought I could save me. But you can't save anyone when you're already dead inside.

I remember the days leading up to her leaving. The gradual unraveling. It wasn't like some dramatic breakup, you know? It wasn't like one of those cliché, movie-style fights with slammed doors and broken glasses. It was slow, deliberate. It was the quiet abandonment that nobody talks about. The moment when you realize you're living with a ghost and not the person you once loved.

I remember her face, pale and tired, sitting at the kitchen table, watching me stumble through the day like a man already buried. She didn't know how to help me, and I didn't know how to help myself. The first time she looked at me with pity, I wanted to throw something. But I couldn't. Because I knew she had a right to pity me. I deserved it. I had destroyed everything we had, piece by piece, until there was nothing left.

I tried to hold onto her, tried to pull her back, but I couldn't. I couldn't stop her. And deep down, I knew she wasn't leaving because she didn't love me anymore. She was leaving because she was tired of trying to love someone who didn't love himself.

Maybe I deserved it. I don't know. But the truth is, I wasn't ready to let go. I didn't know how to let go. And that's when everything got worse. When I realized that love had slipped through my fingers like sand, and I was left with nothing but the hollow sound of my own thoughts echoing in the empty rooms.

The Point of No Return

I still see it—her walking out the door. The last time. Like the moment I knew for sure it was all over, but didn't have the guts to stop it. There was no desperation in her eyes, just a quiet resignation. It wasn't that she hated me, it was that she couldn't love me anymore. It was that simple.

She was packing her things. A few shirts, a couple books, a bottle of perfume—nothing too precious. She didn't even look back when she grabbed her coat, but I could see her. I could see that last glance. A glance that said, "I loved you, but I can't watch you die anymore."

She didn't yell. She didn't beg. She didn't throw the words at me like I expected. She was too tired for that, too broken. I guess I was too. I couldn't even pretend to care. I had my bottle, and that was all I needed.

When she asked me, quietly, "When was the last time you really saw me, Dez?" I didn't have a fucking answer. What was I supposed to say? "I'm sorry"? Sorry for what? Sorry for being the man who couldn't choose between her and my poison? Sorry for the years I wasted drinking her love away until it was just another thing I couldn't touch?

I sat there, numb as usual, watching her leave. I wasn't surprised. I knew it was coming. Hell, I probably knew it from the moment I opened the first can, from the moment I felt the buzz that told me this was easier than dealing with real life. She was just the casualty in a war I was too afraid to fight.

But god, I was still sitting there, holding onto that stupid bottle, pretending that if I just drank enough of it, I could forget her. Forget what I'd lost.

She stopped in the doorway. For a second, I thought maybe she'd turn around. Maybe she'd tell me it was all a mistake, that she'd give me another chance. But she didn't. She just looked at me like I was a stranger, like I was already gone. And maybe I was. She could see what I couldn't. The man I used to be—the one who wanted a life—was long gone.

I remember how the silence settled in after she left. It wasn't the kind of silence that empties the room. It was the kind of silence that fills the room. It packed itself into my chest until I couldn't breathe. I knew, in that moment, that she wasn't coming back. But it wasn't a feeling of regret, not exactly. It was more like I was realizing, finally, that I was the one who didn't deserve to have her.

I kept telling myself I didn't have a choice. That my addiction had taken control, and there was nothing I could do about it. But that was bullshit. I could've chosen. I could've fought. But the fight was too hard, and she was too pure. I'd already burned that bridge long before she ever set her bags down.

So I kept drinking. Because that's all I knew how to do anymore. It wasn't about her. It wasn't even about me. It was about drowning everything—every single thing—so that I didn't have to feel it. Feel the weight of the decision I'd made. Feel the loss that had been too much to face, so I buried it under my own damn misery.

The thing is, I could've changed. I had every chance. Every opportunity to fix it, but I couldn't stop myself. I let the addiction take over, each day, one small step deeper into that black hole, until I couldn't tell what was real anymore. The worst part? I didn't want to. I didn't want to pull myself out. I didn't want to stop hurting.

But now, looking back, I see it. Not just as the loss of her, but as the point of no return. That was the moment I sealed my fate.

The worst part isn't even losing her. It's knowing that I could've been someone else. That I was someone else once, and I threw him away. I could've been the man who made her laugh, who held her at night and told her everything would be alright. I could've been the man who tried. But I wasn't. I wasn't, because I couldn't stop myself from falling into the darkness.

And maybe that's the real truth. That deep down, I didn't want to stop. Maybe I didn't want to be saved, because then I'd have to face all the shit I'd done to get here. To this point where there's no way out. No Ana. No love. Just me, and the hollow fucking hole in my chest that gets bigger with every drink.

The world doesn't care about me, though. Not anymore. I can feel the cold bite of the pavement under my skin, the rustle of forgotten dreams in the gutters. I am the man who has nothing, who lost it all and made peace with it, or pretended to, long ago. I'm the man you walk by on the street and forget, because there's nothing left worth remembering.

She's gone. And I can't go back. Not to her, not to who I used to be. I chose the poison, and now I'm stuck with it.

But here's the thing: I'm not even sure I want to change anymore. Maybe I've become this thing, this shadow of a man, and maybe that's what I am now. Maybe that's what I deserve.

It doesn't matter. The night is cold, and my hands shake as I reach for the bottle. The world is gone. Just me, the liquor, and the quiet scream of my own emptiness.

And it's too late. It's always been too late.

Chapter 7: Life on the Streets

The Routine of Survival

The city's cold, and the morning doesn't care about me. It never does. The sun's not even a hint yet, just the grayness of it pressing down like an apology that isn't coming. I wake up in the usual way—shivering, aching, disoriented. I blink and my eyes don't want to open. I can feel the city pushing against my skull, like it's trying to squeeze me out. I'm not sure if it's the cold or just the weight of being alive.

Another night, another filthy corner in a city that doesn't know I exist. There's a half-crumbled blanket, some food wrappers stuck to my skin, but I don't bother moving them. I'm not here to feel clean, not anymore. I'm here to survive. That's it. Survival's a dirty business. I get it. I wake up from whatever sleep I managed to get, and it feels like the weight of every bad decision I've ever made is sitting on my chest, squeezing my lungs. I don't even know what it's like to wake up somewhere where the air doesn't taste like piss.

I can hear the rattle of the subway below, the hum of it like a ghost moving beneath the streets. It's the only sound that matters. Everything else is noise. The cars, the sirens, the voices—all of it's just a dull roar, like a far-off echo that never really reaches you.

I stretch my legs out, sore and stiff, and roll my blanket up tight. It's not much. It's not even close to enough. But it's mine. A sad little patch of fabric that's seen better days. I've seen better days, too, but they're just memories now, bleeding into the cracks of the streets.

My shoes—if you can call them that—are worn down to the soles. The right one's got a hole in it. The left one's half-falling apart. But they're still holding, so I hold too. It's the only thing left to hold onto.

The day's just starting, but I can already feel the rhythm of it. The way the city moves, relentless and indifferent. People start emerging from the shadows, going from one place to the next, in their own little worlds, pretending they don't see me. They never do. And I've learned to be thankful for that. It's easier this way, not to be seen, not to be a part of their clean little lies.

I drag myself to my feet and shuffle to the corner. There's a deli on the block, the kind of place where the guy behind the counter looks at you like you're a stain on the floor. But I don't care. He knows me by now. Knows that I'll just stand there, waiting, pretending I'm not hoping for the slightest bit of generosity. But the truth is, there's no room for hope anymore. Not here.

I look down at my hands. They're dirty, cracked, rough. I can't remember the last time they weren't like this. I think about Ana sometimes when I look at them. I think about the way she held my hands back then, before the addiction, before everything. Now, it's just a skeleton of what could have been, a ghost of something I can barely remember. I don't know how to reach for something I don't believe in anymore.

I step inside the deli, my eyes scanning for anything that might help—anything to make the day feel like it matters. A sandwich or a cup of coffee. Something warm, at least. But I don't ask. I never ask. You don't beg for scraps here. People have their own troubles to worry about. I'm just a blemish on their nice, neat lives, like a wrinkle in a shirt they can't be bothered to iron out.

The guy behind the counter looks past me, not at me. I stand there for a few minutes, watching him move behind the counter, sliding trays of pre-packaged food onto the shelves, filling the place with the smell of grease and artificial sweetness. I wonder if he knows that he's got everything I don't. He's got a job, a purpose. He's got a future. I don't even have a past anymore.

I walk back out into the street, my stomach empty and the taste of failure already on my tongue. The people in the suits, the ones with the shiny shoes and the slick hair, they pass me by without even a glance. I get it. They've got their own messes to clean up. They're too busy pretending they're going somewhere, too busy making money to worry about a guy like me. It's funny. I used to think I was better than them, that I'd somehow be different. But here I am, sitting in the gutter with the rest of the forgotten ones.

I pull my jacket tighter against my body and keep moving. There's always somewhere to go, somewhere to hide. That's the thing about being invisible. You never have to explain yourself. You don't have to be anything other than what they let you be.

I find a spot by an old church, the kind that's seen better days. The door's open, and I slip inside. It's quiet here, but not peaceful. There's nothing peaceful about a place like this. There's no peace for the lost, no salvation for the ones who can't escape themselves. The floors creak under my weight, and the smell of old incense hangs in the air like a reminder that even the holy can't clean the streets.

I sit in the back, trying to stay out of sight, trying not to be noticed. The pews are empty, and the windows are cracked. The sunlight comes through in jagged streaks, like broken promises, and I close my eyes, wishing I could sleep through it all. But sleep is for the weak, and I can't afford to be weak anymore.

A couple of other homeless people wander in, and I'm glad they don't see me. We've all learned not to look at each other, to pretend we don't know what's happening. We're all just waiting for the next blow to come, the next day to pass. Maybe we'll get lucky. Maybe we won't.

I think about Ana again. I think about how she left. I think about how I let her go, how I chose this. But I'm not sure what else I could have done. I'm not sure there was ever another way. I could have fought. I could have tried. But in the end, it was easier this way. Easier to just slip into the cracks of the city and let the world forget me.

But it doesn't stop. The city doesn't stop. It never does. You keep moving, even if it feels like you're moving in circles. You keep moving, even if you don't know where you're going.

I open my eyes, and the world's still there, still the same. And I'm still here, trying to survive another day.

Dangers and Despair

You ever wake up and just know that something's about to happen? Not in the "I've got a big interview" kind of way, but in the "shit's about to hit the fan" kind of way. The kind of knowing that has nothing to do with luck or fate. It's just the rhythm of the streets. They have their own beat, their own way of telling you when it's time to either move or get moved on.

I woke up to the sound of footsteps. Heavy, uneven. My heart didn't skip a beat, it just kept doing its thing, thumping in the hollow of my chest like it was counting the seconds until it ran out of time.

It was cold, like it always is in the morning, but the kind of cold that grabs your skin and sinks its teeth in deep. I'd found a decent spot under a bridge—dry enough, away from the cops, and not too close to the drunks who sometimes like to use you as a punching bag just for kicks. I don't remember how long I'd been out, but long enough for the smell of stale beer and piss to mix with the damp concrete and make my mouth feel like I'd been chewing on metal.

My eyes cracked open to see a man standing over me. He was taller than me, built like a fucking fridge, his eyes like two dark pits, glaring down, his breath coming out in angry clouds of steam. He stunk of sweat, dirt, and cheap whiskey. The kind of guy who looks at you like you're not human. More like a piece of shit he stepped in and wants to scrape off his boot.

"Got a smoke?" he asked, voice hoarse like he hadn't spoken in days. He was wearing a jacket too nice for the streets, like some rich bastard had thrown it away, and now he was trying to make it look like he belonged in it.

I didn't say anything at first. The air between us felt thick, like the silence had a weight to it. I could feel him staring, waiting for me to respond. He wasn't in any hurry. He didn't need to be.

"No," I finally said. "Don't got a smoke. Don't got anything."

I wasn't lying. I hadn't smoked in weeks. No need for it when you're constantly hungry, constantly chasing that next hit of whatever scraps you can find—food, water, or even just a minute of peace before the next asshole decides to bother you.

He leaned down a little, enough to make me squirm. “I don’t think you understand me,” he said, and I could see it in his eyes. The flicker of something hungry. Not for food, not for money. Something worse.

I scrambled to my feet, half expecting him to pull a knife or worse, but instead, he just reached into his jacket and pulled out a gun. Cold metal shining in the gray morning light. My throat went dry. It wasn’t the first time I’d seen a gun in these parts, but it’s always different when it’s pointed at you.

"Now," he said, voice low, like he was about to tell me a bedtime story. "You’re gonna give me everything you’ve got. Your money, your food, your fucking dignity. You don’t get to say no."

There was something in his voice that didn’t just scare me. It made me feel smaller, like I was beneath him. Like I wasn’t even worth the bullet it would take to end my life.

I looked down at the ground. I had nothing to give. Nothing he could take. But I wasn’t gonna die on my knees. Not like this. Not over nothing.

I tried to look him in the eye, but it was hard. When someone holds a gun at you, your brain doesn’t let you look directly at it. It’s like an invisible force field that bends your focus away. But I looked at him anyway, like I was daring him to make a move.

“You want my stuff, you’re gonna have to take it from me,” I said, and even I didn’t believe the words coming out of my mouth. My heart was racing, pounding like it was about to burst. But something else was going on too. Maybe it was the years of living on this shit-stained sidewalk, maybe it was the anger bubbling under the surface. But I wasn’t backing down.

His face twisted, and for a second, I thought he was gonna pull the trigger. I braced for the pain, for the shock of it. But instead, he started laughing. Big, ugly belly laughs that echoed through the alley, like a sound too dark to come from a human being.

"Funny," he said. "Real funny, man. You think you got something worth taking?"

That was when I saw it. His hand was shaking. Not much, but enough for me to catch it. And maybe it was the desperation in his eyes, maybe it was the sudden realization that he didn't have full control, but I felt it. A crack. A little crack in his power.

I rushed him. It wasn't a plan, just instinct. I dove forward, knocking his arm out of the way just as he fired. The bullet missed, but the blast burned my ear, and I could feel the heat of it in my chest.

We crashed to the ground, my hands grabbing for the gun, his hands trying to shove me off. For a second, it felt like we were the same—both of us just trying to survive, just trying to keep our place in the world.

I didn't know how long we struggled. It felt like a fucking eternity, like everything was happening underwater, slow and distorted. My fingers closed around the barrel of the gun, and I twisted it out of his hand, sending it skittering across the concrete. I heard him scream, but I didn't stop. I kicked him hard in the ribs, again and again, until he stopped moving.

I don't know if I killed him. I didn't care. He didn't matter. He was just another guy who thought he could push me around, another asshole who thought he could own the street just because he had a gun.

When the adrenaline wore off, I stood up, breathing like I had just run a marathon. My body was shaking from the effort, my chest heaving with each breath. The world felt thick again, like it was closing in on me. I hadn't won. It didn't feel like a victory. It just felt like survival.

I looked down at the man on the ground. He was still breathing, his chest rising and falling with each labored breath. And for a moment, I thought about helping him. Maybe dragging him to the side, calling for help. But I knew that wouldn't do anything. I didn't have the energy to care.

So I left. I walked away, feeling the blood pounding in my temples, the cold creeping back in around my shoulders. I didn't look back. I didn't even think about it. I just walked.

I wasn't sure if I was alive anymore, or if I was just stumbling through this nightmare, waiting for the next blow to come.

But one thing I knew—death was always waiting. It wasn't a matter of if. It was when.

A Faint Hope

You ever think maybe you're not supposed to make it? Like, survival itself is a fucking mistake?

I stood there for a moment, still blinking in the sunlight, which felt like it was mocking me—this pale, weak imitation of warmth. People moved around me, their lives marching ahead without a second glance at me. Another street corner, another day. The city didn't stop. It never stopped. It didn't give a shit if you were here or gone, alive or dead.

But then this one guy—this fucking tourist—comes stumbling down the sidewalk. His stupid face bright with that glow that only someone from out of town has, like he's still got hope left in him, like his world isn't already falling apart just like mine.

He's got his camera slung over his neck, looking up at the skyscrapers like they're gods. And he looks at me, for no reason, like I'm something interesting. Like I'm the last fucking unicorn on the planet. He pauses. I see him hesitate.

You see it all the time. They hesitate. Not because they care, but because they don't know what to do with something so ugly, so real. It's like they're checking off some mental list: "Okay, I saw the homeless guy. Don't need to do anything about it. Just checking the box. Next."

But then he reaches into his pocket and pulls out a dollar. Not much. Not even enough to buy a can of beans, but it's something.

"Here," he says, the word coming out like it cost him more than just a dollar. "You... you take care of yourself."

And there it is. The faintest fucking glimmer. For a second, it's like I'm not invisible. Like I'm not just a blot on the landscape.

I can't help it. My fingers twitch for the dollar. I grab it, quick, like it might evaporate. But it doesn't matter. I can feel the edges of it, paper thin, the same way I feel the rest of this world—empty and fragile. He smiles, all eager, waiting for some kind of thanks, and for a split second, I almost give it to him.

But then the rage hits. It's like a fucking wave crashing in. I want to scream at him. Tell him his dollar is worthless. It doesn't change a goddamn thing. It's just a token, a quick little fix to make himself feel better about the way the world is.

What the fuck is a dollar gonna do for me?

I look at him, and for just a second, I almost see something in him—something that doesn't hate. But it's gone before I can hold on to it. I want to say something but my throat is thick, clogged with something I can't name. Something deeper than anger, sharper than bitterness.

I look down at the dollar again, at the paper folds and the fraying edges, and for a second, it feels like I'm holding something more than just cash. Like I'm holding a sliver of something else—something I can't quite touch. Maybe it's hope. Maybe it's a joke. Maybe it's a reminder of something I used to believe.

But it's fleeting. The flicker of humanity. The idea that maybe—just maybe—people aren't all pieces of shit. It burns up fast in the air, like paper too close to a flame.

I snort, laughing bitterly. "Thanks," I mutter, but even the words taste sour.

The tourist doesn't notice. He doesn't care. He just walks off, happy to have done his good deed for the day, checking the box. And I'm left standing there with the dollar in my hand, feeling the weight of it in a way I've never felt anything weigh before. It's light, but heavy. Meaningless, but full of fucking meaning all the same.

I don't know why it hit me this way. Maybe it's the world spinning faster than I can run, or maybe it's that dollar, so small and meaningless to him but somehow too much for me to carry.

I want to throw it away. Throw it in his face. Scream at him, "You think this makes a difference? You think you gave me hope?"

But the words die before they can leave my mouth. They get stuck in the pit of my stomach, where all the anger and desperation are folded up like a tight ball of paper, just waiting to be lit on fire.

I take the dollar, fold it, shove it in my pocket, and walk away. The day continues its relentless march forward, indifferent to whether I'm still here or not.

I know what people expect. I know what they think when they see me. They think they've got it figured out. "Another junkie. Another lost cause. Just some asshole who's too weak to get his shit together."

But the truth? The fucking truth is that it's not about strength. It's not about who has what, who can scrape by longer, or who's tougher. It's about who can keep pretending, and who can't.

I stand there in the middle of the street, watching the cars fly by, watching people scurry, like ants, unaware of the enormous weight of life they're all carrying.

What's the point of all this? What's the point of getting up every day just to survive, just to scrape by until the next round of shit comes slamming into your face? What's the point of it?

I used to think if I could just make it out of this—if I could just get my hands on something better—maybe, just maybe, I could find a way out. But now? Now, I'm not sure. I'm not sure if there's a way out. Or if it even matters.

A HAPPY DEATH

I've spent my whole life chasing things—chasing hope, chasing a better life, chasing something that makes the shit feel worthwhile. And all I've got to show for it is a few empty bottles and a goddamn dollar in my pocket that won't make a goddamn difference.

It's easy to see why people give up. It's easy to just stop pretending that things are going to get better. The city's full of people who've lost that fight. They don't tell you they've lost. They just don't care anymore.

And that's the thing they don't get. When you've been on the streets long enough, when you've seen everything that there is to see, you start to see the cracks in the system. You see the whole thing is a farce. People fighting for scraps, pretending like they matter, like any of it means anything.

But there's nothing new about this fight. The system's rigged. Always has been. Always will be. People get knocked down, and they stay down. They get used up, tossed aside, and told that they failed, that they didn't try hard enough. Like they didn't deserve better.

I don't think about the dollar anymore.

Instead, I think about how long this cycle is going to go on. How many more people are gonna end up here, in the dirt, in the cold, holding out their hands for scraps of something that doesn't even exist.

And maybe the worst part? Maybe the real punchline in all this? Is that somewhere deep down, I think I'm supposed to care. I think I'm supposed to believe in that glimmer of hope. But every time I try, it just slips away. Like trying to hold water in your hands.

I walk the streets, but I'm not going anywhere. I just keep moving because that's all I can do. The world is too loud, too fast for me to catch up. The dollar's still in my pocket. Maybe it's a reminder, maybe it's just another thing weighing me down.

But at least it's something. Even if it doesn't mean a damn thing.

Chapter 8: More Encounters with Marie

Marie's Persistence

She's back. That Marie.

It's the same routine: she appears like clockwork, looking at me with that look—the one that wants to erase every stain on the world with a half-smile and a limp, misplaced act of kindness. Her hands are full of cheap, used-up mittens, holding a paper cup of warm water like it's supposed to mean something, like I'm supposed to be grateful for it.

I don't want the water. I don't need it. But I take it anyway. I can feel the heat of it through the paper, like it's trying to thaw some part of me that's been buried too deep for too long. I stare at it, waiting for her to say something. She always does. She doesn't know when to leave me the fuck alone.

"Here, Dez," she says, like it's some big thing, like she's saving my life with a fucking cup of water. "You should come with me. Come to the shelter. It's not far. They've got a warm bed. A hot meal. You don't have to stay forever, just... just think about it. Think about it, okay?"

Shelter. Help. I know that game. I've played it too many times to fall for it again. It's always the same. You walk in, they give you some shitty blankets and a meal, and then you're supposed to feel like you owe them your fucking soul. They can't fix me. Nobody can.

I don't answer right away. I just watch the steam curl off the water. It's like I can see my own breath in it. Like the warmth from the cup is trying to crawl back into my bones. But there's nothing left inside me to warm. There's just the cold.

"You keep doing this," I finally say, looking up at her. "What the fuck do you think you're gonna fix? You think you can save me? You think you can fix whatever the hell's broken inside me with a cup of water and some bullshit about a warm bed?"

I try to keep my voice low, calm. I'm not trying to yell at her, but the words are coming anyway, like bile in the back of my throat. I can feel the anger simmering, thick in my chest. I don't need her pity. I don't need her trying to save me.

She stands there, like she always does, those mittens wrapped around the cup. Her face doesn't change. She doesn't flinch. She just looks at me, like I'm not a mess on the sidewalk, like I'm just some guy who needs a little push to remember what it's like to be human.

"Dez," she says, her voice steady, her eyes fixed on mine. "I'm not trying to save you. I'm just trying to show you that you don't have to do this alone. You don't have to live this way."

I laugh, bitter, low. "Alone?" I say, like she doesn't know the fucking meaning of the word. "I've been alone my whole life. The difference is, I'm not asking for your fucking help. I'm not asking for anyone's help. You can't fix this. You can't fix me."

The words hit her, and for a second, I think I've broken her. I think I've said the one thing that'll make her go away and never come back. That's what I want. I don't need her standing here, offering me false hope, making me feel like I'm worth saving.

But she doesn't go away. She doesn't even blink.

"You're wrong," she says, almost quietly. "You're wrong about that."

I don't know why, but something in her voice catches me off guard. It's not the usual pity or concern. It's just... something else. Like she's talking to a person, not a goddamn charity case. And I fucking hate it.

I slam the cup down on the ground. It bounces once, then tumbles to the gutter, water spilling out into the filth. I feel that empty space inside me flare up. I want to tell her to go to hell. I want to tell her that she doesn't get it, that no one gets it, that nothing changes and nothing ever will.

"You don't understand," I say, my voice shaking. "There's nothing left to fix. There's nothing good about me. I'm just a fucking mess, and that's all I'll ever be. I've been out here too long, Marie. I've been broken too long for anyone to put back together."

She doesn't back off. She steps closer. I can smell her now—soap and something clean, something I'll never touch again. It stings my nose. It makes my teeth ache. I want to shove her away. I want to scream at her to leave, to go back to her little life and forget I ever existed.

But she doesn't back off.

"You don't have to fix everything," she says, her voice low but firm. "You just have to take one step. One small step. Just... one."

And for a moment—just a moment—I almost believe her. I almost think maybe, just maybe, I could take that step. Maybe I could walk away from all this. Maybe I could be something else. But I know it's not true. I know better than to believe in that shit.

"Step?" I snort. "You think I can just walk away from all this?" I gesture at the street, at the shit-stained concrete, the noise, the smell, the filth that's swallowed me whole. "What the hell's a step gonna do? It's just gonna get buried under more bullshit. I'm too far gone for that."

I don't wait for her response. I turn away, because I can't stand the way she's looking at me, like she sees something I can't see, like she sees some version of me that doesn't exist. It makes my skin crawl. It makes me feel like I'm falling into a hole I can't get out of.

"You think a fucking bed and some hot food is gonna fix me?" I say over my shoulder, my voice cracking with the weight of it. "You think that's gonna fix the shit in my head? It doesn't work like that. It never works."

But she's not backing down. I can feel her eyes on my back, boring into me like she's waiting for me to say something else. Like she's waiting for me to admit that maybe, just maybe, I want to believe in her.

But I won't. I can't. I've been here too long. I've seen too much. And I know how this story ends. There's no escape.

"Marie," I say, my voice low, raw, and tired. "I'm not asking for your fucking help."

She doesn't say anything. She just watches me, like she's waiting for something to break.

I don't break. I walk away.

I don't look back. I don't have the energy to.

And for just a second, I wish I could.

The Resistance

Marie didn't leave me alone.

I hated her for it. I don't know what made her keep coming back—maybe she thought it was her personal mission to "save" me, maybe she didn't know any better, or maybe she just needed to believe she could make a difference. I could see it in the way she looked at me, that soft, pitying gaze that made me feel like something less than a man. I wasn't some fucking pet. I wasn't some stray she could take home and feed and make better. She didn't get it.

The first time she came back, I was huddled under a filthy cardboard box, the kind you only see in movies about poverty, except this wasn't a movie—it was my life. And life out here doesn't have a soundtrack or happy endings. It's just the cold concrete, the piss-soaked streets, and the noise of a city that doesn't care about you.

"Dez," she called out, too brightly, as if the sun was still shining in her world. "I brought you something. You can't just stay under there all day. You need to get warm."

I didn't even look up. I didn't want to. I didn't want her pity, or her food, or whatever fucking charity she was trying to hand me. Her voice grated on me, making my stomach churn. She looked out of place—shiny coat, thick hair, too much kindness. I wanted to make her feel as small as I felt, to remind her that she didn't belong in my world.

"I don't need it," I muttered, my voice cracked and sharp. "I don't need your fucking help."

She crouched down in front of me, not a hint of hesitation in her movements. She had that look again—the one where she thought I was just some project, some sad broken thing waiting for her to come along and fix it. It made me sick. "I've got a blanket for you. Some dry clothes." Her hand extended, like it was some offer of salvation, and I wanted to scream at her. I wasn't a fucking charity case.

"I said no," I barked, louder this time. "I don't want it."

She didn't pull back. She didn't flinch. It's like she didn't hear the words coming out of my mouth. She just stayed there, waiting for me to cave, to let myself be saved. I could feel the heat of her, even through the grime and the cold, and I wanted to crawl inside my own skin and hide from it.

"Marie," I growled, "you don't get it. I'm too far gone. Don't waste your time. I don't need your fucking charity."

She didn't say anything for a while. I could hear the wind pick up, the city pulsing with its usual cacophony of life moving on without me. When she finally spoke, her voice was softer, like she knew I was breaking, but she didn't know how to stop it. "I'm not asking you to come with me forever, Dez. Just one night. A warm bed. A meal. Please, just take a step."

I could feel something in me twist, like a rope pulling tighter. Goddamn it, why did she have to do this to me? I could feel the weight of her words, pressing on me like I had some obligation to accept her hand, to trust in something I hadn't trusted in years. A part of me wanted to believe her. That tiny, stupid part that still thought there was a way out of this mess. But I knew better. I wasn't going to walk into some shelter like it was a fucking rescue mission. I wasn't going to be saved. Not by her. Not by anyone.

"I'm not that guy," I said, barely above a whisper, my voice trembling with the weight of something I didn't want to admit to myself. "I'm not worth it. I'm beyond saving."

Her eyes didn't break. They just held me, like she was waiting for me to see something in her that would finally make me understand. But I wasn't ready to see it. Not yet. "Dez," she said, her voice thick with something like grief, "I'm not asking you to be fixed. I'm asking you to take one step. Just one. Please."

It hit me harder than I expected. One step. One fucking step. How many times had I been given chances to change, to stop running, to step into something that could make me feel alive again? But I couldn't do it. I couldn't move. I was stuck in this hole I'd dug for myself, and I wasn't ready to climb out.

"Marie," I said, my hands shaking, "I can't."

I don't know if I meant that I couldn't take the step, or if I meant I couldn't believe she was still standing there, trying to pull me out of this mess.

But I couldn't.

She stood up then, slowly, like she was giving up on me but not on the idea of me. Like I was a lost cause but still somehow worth her time. She didn't argue. She didn't try to change my mind. She just held the blanket and the clothes for a second longer, and then—without another word—she walked away. Her footsteps echoed in my chest, the sound of someone leaving me behind. But it wasn't just her. It was me too.

The second time, she came back.

The wind had picked up by then, slicing through the alleys, turning the city into a cold, uncaring machine. I was in the same place, slumped against the cold stone of some shitty apartment building, my back sore, my stomach empty. I don't know why I stayed in the same spot. Maybe it was because I wanted her to come back. Maybe I wanted to prove something to myself, that I wasn't the kind of man who let hope slip through his fingers. Maybe I wanted to prove to myself that I could still reject her.

"Dez," she said, kneeling down again, the sound of her voice different now. It wasn't pleading, it was tired. "I brought you some coffee. Something warm."

Her hands were shaking. She wasn't trying to hide it anymore. She was just trying to get me to see what I didn't want to see—that even after everything I'd said, everything I'd pushed away, she was still offering.

"I don't want it," I said again, but this time the words felt wrong. They didn't feel like a defense anymore. They felt like a lie.

"You're freezing," she said, her breath fogging in front of her. She was right, but I wasn't going to admit it. "Dez, just take a step. You can't keep living like this."

And that was when it happened—the thing I'd been avoiding for so long. I felt a flicker. A flicker of something. Not hope, not yet. But the thought that maybe, just maybe, I wasn't as far gone as I'd convinced myself I was. The thought that, maybe, I could take that one step. But I shut it down. Hard.

"I'm too fucked up for that," I muttered, looking away.

She didn't say anything after that. She just stood there for a while, like she was waiting for me to see it, but I couldn't. Not yet. I wasn't ready to let her in.

"Okay," she said, after what felt like hours. "Okay, Dez. But I'll keep coming back. You don't have to take that step, but I'll be here. Every time."

I didn't reply. I didn't need to. She'd already made her choice. But I knew, somewhere deep down, that I hadn't made mine yet.

A Quiet Connection

I sit there, in the cold that claws at your bones like it's trying to remind you you're still alive, even if you wish you weren't. The streets of New York hum around me, but tonight they feel quieter. The air's thin—humid even though it's late, thick with the grime of the city. Car exhausts mix with the distant sound of sirens and the low, muffled thrum of life going on without me. Marie is gone for the night, but her footsteps, those soft, tentative steps, are still echoing in my head.

The note weighs heavy in my pocket. Not because it's anything important, but because it's everything I'm not. Everything I used to be, maybe. Something small, something kind, something I don't deserve. That's what it feels like. A lie.

I pull it out now, slowly, like a man pulling a tooth he knows should come out but can't quite bring himself to do it. The paper crinkles between my fingers, thin and fragile, the same way I feel every time I look at it. A phone number. A message scrawled in a hand that isn't mine: "If you change your mind, I'll be here. You're not alone." It's not much. In fact, it's almost nothing. But the words tear at me, scraping against the black hole I keep locked inside.

A soft breeze stirs the crumpled paper, sending it fluttering in my hands, but I don't move. My eyes stay fixed on the numbers, the fading ink that's already starting to blur under the humidity of the air. I try to focus, to make sense of what she said, but it keeps slipping away, like I'm trying to hold onto a shadow.

"You're not alone," she said.

I chuckle bitterly, the sound lost in the distant rumble of a passing subway. Not alone? Hell, I'm more alone than anyone could ever understand. Not alone? The only thing I'm not alone with is the stench of sweat and piss and garbage and regret. The only voice I hear is my own, the one inside my head, telling me I've crossed too many lines to turn back now.

But still—still, I can't make myself throw it away. I sit there with the paper in my hand, my fingertips pressing into the corners like I'm trying to erase it. But it won't go. It won't leave me.

I hear her voice again, softer this time, as though it's coming from inside my chest. *"You're not alone."* I hate it. I hate it because it's true, and I don't want it to be.

I'm not sure how long I sit there. The city moves around me, but I stay frozen, stuck in the space between despair and something else. Something I don't have the words for. Something I can't name.

The moon hangs low in the sky, heavy and white. It's too damn close, like it's watching me. It doesn't blink. I stare up at it, the cold light washing over the concrete, and it makes me feel like an insect under a magnifying glass. I can almost feel the weight of it on my shoulders, pressing down, reminding me how small and insignificant I am in the vastness of everything.

I think about Marie again. How she walked away, looking back over her shoulder, leaving me here with the damn note. Maybe she thinks she's helping. Maybe she really believes in all that hope and kindness bullshit. But what does she know about this life? What does she know about sitting on the curb, half-drunk on your own mistakes, with nothing but the wind and the sound of your own thoughts to keep you company?

I run the paper between my fingers, tracing the numbers, the same way I trace the scars on my hands. I don't know why I keep them. The scars, the note—they don't matter. Nothing does. What's the point of saving a man who doesn't want to be saved?

I laugh, but it's a hollow sound, swallowed by the streetlights and the hum of the traffic. And for a second, just a second, I wonder if Marie would still be here if I'd said yes. If I'd gone with her. If I'd taken that damn blanket, let her wrap me in it like I was something worth saving. I wonder if there was a time when I thought I deserved saving.

I don't look at the note anymore. I fold it up and slip it back in my jacket pocket. I don't know if I'm going to keep it or throw it away. I don't know if I'll ever call her. I don't know anything anymore. Not about people, not about the city, not about what I'm doing here, or why I'm still breathing.

But somehow, the paper stays with me. It stays in my pocket, tucked close to my chest like a whisper I can't ignore.

I stand up slowly, the chill creeping into my bones, and for the first time tonight, I don't feel quite so heavy. The night is still alive, full of traffic, and trash, and broken promises. The moon still hovers above, indifferent to everything down here. But maybe, just maybe, I'm not quite as far gone as I thought.

I turn my back on the alley, and for a moment, I think I can hear the sound of my footsteps echoing in the distance, as if the city is telling me that I'm still here. Not gone. Not yet.

And I keep walking.

Chapter 9: Stevie's Introduction

The Jaded Survivor

The first time I saw Stevie, I thought he was just another fucking zombie on the corner—some ghost of a man, worn out from too many winters on the streets, too many pills, too many fights, too many cigarettes burned down to the filter. He sat on a cracked milk crate, slouched back against a flickering lamppost, looking like he'd been there for an eternity. He didn't look at anyone. Didn't even blink. Just sucked in smoke, deep, like he was drinking the last sip from a bottle long gone dry.

I thought he'd never notice me—hell, he didn't look like he noticed anything. But something about him kept pulling me back, like a cold magnet. Like he was the last of something that was almost gone, but not quite dead yet. I started walking past him every day. Same time. Same spot. At first, he didn't say a word to me. Just let me be another set of footsteps in the street.

I'd watch him from the corner of my eye. He'd just sit there, doing nothing. Like a carcass on display for the vultures, who never came. He wasn't begging. He wasn't looking for a handout. He was waiting for something, but I couldn't figure out what. Maybe he was waiting for his heart to stop. Maybe he was waiting for his soul to catch up to the rot of his body.

Weeks passed, and I started to hate the sight of him. Not because he was a reminder of what I could become—but because he had already fucking become it, and the worst part was, he didn't seem to care. I had my pride. I told myself I wasn't like him, that I wasn't giving up yet. I wasn't gonna let the street swallow me whole.

But then one night, Stevie spoke to me.

"You're gonna get yourself killed if you keep walking around like that," he said, his voice cracked, rough, like someone had scraped gravel against his vocal cords for fun.

I stopped in my tracks. I wasn't ready for this. I wasn't ready for him to see me. To see how I had stopped pretending. How I was starting to look just like him.

"What the hell's that supposed to mean?" I shot back, but I could feel the words slipping out of me like I was trying to crawl back into my own skin.

He didn't look up. Just took a drag off his cigarette, slowly, like he had all the time in the world. Then, like he wasn't even talking to me, like he was just thinking out loud: "The street's got a way of chewing you up. People see you, sure. They walk by. They act like they can't hear you. But then, one day, it's not just the city that's swallowed you. It's you that's swallowed. You're gonna turn into one of these stones on the sidewalk, just waiting for someone to step on you and keep walking."

I felt the weight of his words like a stone in my gut. He didn't look at me. Didn't pity me. Didn't care about my story. Just a man who'd already let go of everything, looking at the world through dead eyes.

"Who the hell are you to tell me that?" I snapped.

"Doesn't matter who I am," Stevie said, his voice low, uninterested. "What matters is whether you're still alive tomorrow. Or if you're gonna be another fool who thought he could keep his morals in a place like this. The streets don't care about that. You got a code or a conscience out here? Good luck keeping it. Ain't nothing but a noose for the weak."

That's when I knew—there was no compassion left in him. No dreams. No ideals. Just survival. And survival, in Stevie's world, meant you did whatever you had to do, regardless of who you stepped on. In his world, you were nothing but meat. And it wasn't enough to just stay alive. You had to stay alive longer than the next guy.

So, over the next few days, I started to watch Stevie more closely. I didn't just walk past him anymore. I sat down beside him. I didn't ask questions. I just listened. He didn't have the energy to talk much. When he did speak, it was in bursts—short and blunt, like each word had been pulled from his throat with a rusted hook.

One night, he showed me how to survive out here, in the only way he knew how.

Stevie took me to a small liquor store, tucked between two rundown buildings, its windows filthy with years of neglect. He didn't knock or ask permission—he just walked in like he owned the place. I stood at the door, half-watching, half-afraid.

He walked straight up to the counter, grabbed a bottle of cheap bourbon, and slipped it into his jacket. The clerk didn't even flinch. Stevie didn't say a word. Just nodded to the guy behind the counter like they'd done this dance a thousand times before. Then, he turned and walked out.

"You see?" Stevie said as we stepped back into the night air, the bottle heavy in his coat. "You think you can beg for a dollar, or put on some sad story and hope someone gives a shit? That's cute, kid. But that ain't how you make it out here."

I felt a tightness in my chest. I wasn't sure if it was shame or something else—something darker.

"What if we get caught?"

Stevie didn't laugh. He didn't even look at me. "You either get away with it, or you get caught. Ain't no in-between. Ain't no second chances. The moment you stop thinking like that, the moment you start believing someone's gonna come and save you, that's the moment you stop breathing. We don't get saved out here. We don't get nothing."

He was right. And somehow, that made it worse. Because I could feel myself slipping. I could feel my humanity starting to peel away, layer by layer, like I was shedding my own skin. And Stevie? He was already fucking gone.

He showed me how to hustle for food, how to read the signs of a mark, how to beg without being too obvious, how to take what I could, when I could, without ever looking back. He taught me how to survive on the streets—not like a person, but like a scavenger, like a parasite living off whatever scraps life threw at us.

After a while, I wasn't sure if I was learning from him or just turning into him. I wasn't sure if it mattered anymore.

There was a twisted comfort in it, though. It was the comfort of knowing there were no questions, no expectations. The world had already been stripped away, and the only thing left was the raw, unfiltered truth. We weren't people anymore. We were just survivors, getting by day by day. And maybe, just maybe, that was the only thing that mattered.

Life's Futility

I used to think I was different from Stevie. I thought I had something he didn't—some kind of fire that burned inside me, something to fight for. Maybe it was my youth. Maybe it was the hope that hadn't been completely ground out of me. But after a few weeks with Stevie, I could see it in his eyes—he wasn't just a street-rat; he was a ghost who had already died. The city had swallowed him whole, and now he was just waiting for the body to catch up. I could see it in the way he moved, slow and deliberate, like a man who had nothing left to prove and no place to go.

One night, we sat on the same milk crate. I was cold, like I always was by this time of year. The wind in the city cuts right through you. Stevie didn't seem to notice. He had this way of ignoring the world around him, like he was already dead to it, and it had no use for him either.

"You know why I'm still here?" Stevie asked, looking at me sideways. His cigarette dangled between his lips like it had a purpose, but Stevie never did anything for a reason. Not anymore.

I waited, but didn't answer. I couldn't tell him that I wasn't sure what the hell I was still doing here either. Sometimes, it felt like I was just passing time, not living it.

"Because I've got nothing to lose," Stevie said, like the words didn't mean anything to him. "Nothing. And it's the one thing this city can't take away."

His words hit me like a slap. He didn't want to be here. But here he was. And I wasn't sure if he was hanging on to life anymore or if he had just stopped caring. He didn't beg. Didn't talk to anyone. The only thing he did was survive. And that was all that mattered.

"You think you're still fighting?" he asked, his voice steady, almost like he wasn't talking to me anymore, but to the concrete beneath us. "You think you're gonna win? Kid, this city doesn't lose. The system doesn't lose. People like you and me? We're just parts of the system. We're the forgotten ones. The rats in the walls, the trash in the gutter. We're disposable."

I wanted to argue, to say something that would prove that I wasn't like him. That I wasn't ready to be buried alive in this city, to become one of its lost souls. But I couldn't. His words stuck with me like rotting meat.

"Then why not just give up?" I finally asked, the question slipping out before I could stop it. "Why keep going?"

Stevie took a long drag from his cigarette, exhaling the smoke like he was pushing out a lifetime's worth of regrets. He didn't even look at me when he spoke. His eyes were dead, locked somewhere far beyond the cracked sidewalks, beyond the dirty streets. He was looking at something I couldn't see.

"You give in," he said, his voice flat, void of hope. "You stop fighting. And it stops hurting."

I wanted to scream at him, to tell him he was wrong. That there had to be something more to life than just surviving. But I didn't. Because deep down, I knew he was right. The longer I stayed out here, the more I felt like I was turning into one of those ghosts. The city had a way of doing that to you. Of taking everything and leaving you with nothing but your own skin and bones, a mind that couldn't shut off, and a soul that could barely feel anymore.

"What does it feel like?" I asked, not sure if I even wanted to know the answer. "To stop caring?"

Stevie finally turned his head, his face an unreadable mask of indifference. "It feels like freedom," he said, the words so empty that they made my stomach twist. "It feels like you've finally let go of the weight of the world. It's the only peace you'll find out here."

I wanted to argue. I wanted to shout that I still had a spark, something worth fighting for. But the longer I stayed with Stevie, the more I started to see the truth in what he was saying. Out here, there wasn't any room for dreams. There wasn't any space for hope. There was just the street, the people who walked by like they couldn't see you, the ones who threw a dollar at you like they were doing you a favor. And there was the ever-present gnawing in your gut—the hunger, the cold, the desperation that never let you forget you were nothing more than a cog in the machine.

The city didn't care if you lived or died. It didn't care if you had a name, a past, or a future. It just kept on moving, grinding you down, until you were as much a part of the concrete as the filth in the gutters.

"You can fight all you want," Stevie said, tapping his cigarette against the crate, sending a thin plume of ash to the ground. "But the city wins. The system wins. It's all just one big game, and we're all just pieces on the board. You think you can change it? Nah. You can't. You can't beat it. So you learn to survive, and you stop caring. You let the game play you, instead of trying to play it. And that's when you stop hurting."

I sat there, the cold sinking into my bones, the weight of his words pressing down on me. Part of me wanted to reject everything he said. But another part of me, the part that had been out here too long, knew that Stevie was right. The city had broken me before I even had a chance to break it.

I couldn't escape it. None of us could.

But maybe, just maybe, if I stopped fighting, if I just let myself slip into the nothingness like Stevie had, I could stop feeling like I was constantly drowning. Maybe I could stop fighting for something that was never going to come.

I looked at Stevie then, really looked at him. His face was lined with a hundred years of street life. His eyes, dull and tired, held nothing but resignation. But there was something in him I couldn't name. Something that made him seem like he was in control of his own emptiness. And for a moment, I wanted that. I wanted to let go of the fight. I wanted to surrender.

"Does it ever feel... better?" I asked, unsure of what I was hoping for.

Stevie's lips twitched slightly, like the question amused him. "It doesn't feel anything," he said. "And that's the best part."

I let the silence fall between us. I wasn't sure if I wanted to be like him, but the thought was there, lingering in the back of my mind. The thought that maybe, just maybe, if I gave up on fighting the city, if I let it win, maybe the pain would stop. Maybe the cold, the hunger, the loneliness wouldn't hurt so much anymore.

But I knew one thing—whether I chose to keep fighting or not, it was already too late. The city had already swallowed me whole.

The Changing Perspective

Stevie's got this way of walking. Like he's floating. Like he's part of the pavement, part of the grime, part of everything, and nothing at the same time. His steps are slow, deliberate—like he's already seen everything, like there's nothing left to know, and the rest of the world can just keep spinning. The city passes him by like he's invisible. Hell, maybe he is. I don't know anymore.

I watch him out of the corner of my eye, this old man in a coat that smells like stale piss and cheap whiskey. His face is all creased like a crumpled paper bag, eyes that've looked at too much, felt too little. His lips twist into this permanent sneer, but it ain't anger anymore. It's indifference. And somehow, that makes more sense than all the fire I've been carrying around inside me.

We don't talk much. We don't need to. The silence between us has become its own language. It's not the kind of silence where you feel awkward, like you've got something to hide. Nah, this is the silence of two souls who've stopped pretending that there's anything left to save. The city's loud enough for both of us.

"You can fight all you want," Stevie tells me one night, voice rasping like old paper. "But the city wins. The system wins. You're just a part of it, a forgotten part." He takes a drag from his cigarette and flicks the ash onto the ground, as if that's what all this is: just trash, burning away to nothing. "So stop giving a shit about it."

I stare at him, but I don't feel the urge to scream like I did before. Something in his voice is like a needle poking into a wound I didn't know I had. And for the first time, I feel it. The truth of it. He's not wrong.

It's hard to explain, but there's this sudden weight lifting off my chest. Maybe because I've been fighting for too long. Fighting for what? A life that doesn't exist? I don't know. But there's this quiet relief in his words, like someone telling you that the fight was rigged from the start and you were never going to win. So why bother?

The world keeps moving around us—sirens, car horns, the low hum of the subway, the noise of a thousand lives rushing by. But it's all background. It doesn't matter anymore.

I start following Stevie, watching the way he moves through the streets. He doesn't look at people. Hell, he doesn't even see them. He just keeps going. Like he's already dead. Maybe he is. I don't know. Maybe we all are. What difference does it make?

Every night, I sit with him on the corner, feeling the chill crawl up my spine. We don't say much. I ask him questions, but he just gives me these short answers. He doesn't have much to say anymore. Hell, maybe I don't either.

But I keep asking anyway. It's like a habit I can't shake. Like I need something to hold onto, even if it's just words, even if they don't mean a damn thing.

"Do you ever think about getting out?" I ask him one night, as the shadows stretch longer across the sidewalk, cold fingers creeping into the cracks of the city.

He stops, looks at me for a long time, like he's trying to remember what it means to care. Then he shakes his head. "Out?" he mutters. "Out of what? The city? Or your head?"

It hits me all at once. The city isn't just the buildings, the streets, the noise. It's the air we breathe. It's the stuff that gets inside your veins. You can't run from it. You can't escape it. You can't leave it behind. You just become part of it. A part of the dust, the grime, the noise. The city gets inside you and twists you into shapes you never wanted to be.

I start seeing it, start seeing everything differently. People passing by—rushing, not looking at anyone, eyes locked straight ahead. They don't see me. They don't see Stevie. They don't see anyone. We're all invisible. I guess we always were.

Stevie doesn't care. That's the thing. He's stopped caring. And I'm starting to think that maybe that's the only way to survive. Not by fighting. Not by begging or stealing or dreaming about some day when things are better. No. You survive by accepting it. By letting it eat you whole. By letting it take everything and asking for more.

We steal when we need to, but it's not like it matters. We're just taking back what's ours, what the city's already stolen from us. It's not about guilt or morals. It's about surviving the day. We don't steal because we're bad people. We steal because the system's already rigged, and you might as well get yours while you can.

Stevie taught me that. How to live without hope. How to breathe without wanting. How to walk through the streets and be nothing, feel nothing, but still keep going.

And then one morning, he didn't show up.

I waited on the corner where we always met, but Stevie never came. I waited for days, but there was no sign. I asked around, but nobody had seen him. They don't care, you know? The people in the street, the ones that pass us by. They don't care about the lost souls who shuffle through their lives. And Stevie? He was just another lost soul.

I thought I'd feel something. I thought I'd feel like I'd lost a friend, a mentor, hell, even a father. But I didn't. I felt nothing.

The city kept moving. The world didn't stop turning. And that's when I realized what Stevie had been telling me all along: life is nothing but a chain of movements. You survive. You breathe. You move. You die. And no one gives a damn. Not really.

So, I keep moving. Not because I think there's a point. Not because I'm trying to fix anything. I keep moving because that's all there is. The city wins. It always wins. And I'm just another part of it. Another cog in the machine, grinding away until I'm nothing but dust.

Chapter 10: Flashbacks of the Past

The Beginning of the End

The story changes every time I think of her.

I remember her smile like it was a knife. A smile that cut through all the bullshit I used to tell myself. A smile that could've been the start of something. But the problem with smiles like that is they don't last. You get used to the good moments, and then it's the bad ones that dig in and stay, like little splinters under your skin.

Ana was never perfect. She had that broken kind of beauty—messed-up hair, eyes that looked like they'd seen too much for someone so young. But when she looked at me, it felt like the world could be different. Like we could be different. I thought I was worthy of that love. I thought I could be someone else with her—someone who didn't need a needle to feel alive. But I was wrong.

The first time we went out, she laughed at something stupid I said. She laughed like she meant it, like I wasn't just a joke with bad jokes, like I wasn't already halfway dead. I never wanted to be the kind of guy who needed someone to save him, but I could tell right then that she saw me as someone worth saving. And that's when I knew I'd fuck it all up.

We used to talk about getting away—just the two of us, away from the city, away from everything that kept us tied to this shit. We'd talk about places—maybe somewhere on the edge of nowhere, where the world couldn't touch us, where I wouldn't need a fix just to feel the sun on my skin. I could see it in her eyes, that kind of dream we both shared. I could hear it in the way she said, "What if we just disappeared? What if we didn't have to play their game anymore?"

It was all talk, of course. I was good at that. Talk, talk, talk. Make the words smooth enough to convince myself that I was really capable of change. But in the end, it's just noise. Words like "tomorrow" and "we" and "hope" are only useful until you hit the bottom and realize they're not real. And I hit the bottom faster than I ever thought possible.

I didn't even notice when she stopped believing in me. It was like a slow fade, a slow unraveling. One day, she was sitting there, holding my hand, telling me she loved me. The next, she was looking at me like she was already a stranger. I remember her hands shaking. I wanted to grab her, make her see that I was still me, that I wasn't the person I'd become. But I was too deep in it. Too deep in the haze of the needle, the high that would make me forget everything I didn't want to feel.

She tried. She really did. Ana didn't walk away easily. She kept coming back, again and again, her love a lifeline thrown out to someone who was too busy drowning to even try and grab it. I remember one night, we were sitting on the floor of the apartment. She had made dinner. It wasn't much, but she'd cooked it for us. I could see her looking at me like she was trying to figure out who I was—trying to figure out if there was any of the man she once loved left in me.

I could see it, too. The guilt, the shame, the loss that had started to settle inside me. I felt like I was fading away right in front of her. She kept asking me if I was okay, if I wanted help. And I kept lying. It was easier to lie. It was easier to smile, to tell her that it wasn't as bad as it looked. But the truth is, I had nothing left to give her. Nothing but promises that tasted like ash.

The first time she left, I didn't think much of it. I was numb, as usual. She said she was going to visit her mom for a few days. That was the first time she told me she needed some space. I didn't think it was a big deal. I figured she'd come back. She always came back.

But she didn't. Not this time.

I remember sitting in that apartment, the walls closing in, the silence so thick it was like I could taste it. I sat there for hours, maybe days, just staring at the empty space where she used to be. Her scent still hung in the air. I couldn't even tell if I missed her or if I was just missing the idea of someone loving me. There's a difference. But when you're high, when you're buried in it, you don't really think about what's real.

She came back a few more times after that, but I wasn't the same anymore. The addict had taken me fully, and I couldn't even pretend to be the man I once was. I wasn't even the same man I was the day before. Each hit changed me just a little bit more. I could see it in her eyes, too—she didn't want to admit it, but I could see the hurt in the way she looked at me. The way she stayed even though she knew it was pointless. It was like watching someone trying to save a drowning man who refused to float.

One day, she just... left. For good. I don't even know if I said goodbye. I don't remember. I was probably too busy chasing that next high, that next moment of numbness. It wasn't a grand exit. There were no tears. No big confrontation. Just a few words that were easy to say, but so goddamn hard to hear.

"I can't do this anymore, Dez. I can't save you."

And that was it. She was gone.

I don't know how long I stayed in that place after she left. Days? Weeks? It doesn't matter. Time doesn't mean shit when you're a junkie. I wasn't living, I was just existing. But the thing about existing is that you can't keep it up forever. Eventually, your body gives out. Eventually, your soul wears thin.

I never blamed her for leaving. How could I? Who could blame anyone for leaving a wreck like me? But that doesn't make it hurt any less. It just makes the pain feel more real, like I earned it somehow.

The Downward Spiral

Sometimes I think it would've been easier if I'd just stayed face down in that gutter. But I never did. I crawled out of it, over and over, like some half-assed zombie. It's always harder when you know you could've been something else. That's what she did to me, Ana. She showed me a glimpse of something I didn't deserve—a life with light in it, one that wasn't just dirty, or drunk, or high. We talked about futures we had no business imagining. Dreams of a house in the country, a porch swing, and a dog. You know, the bullshit they try to sell you in movies. I told her it was all garbage. But it felt good to believe it for a second. God, it felt good.

She was the kind of woman who saw a future even in me. I should've known that was too good to be true. A guy like me can only hang onto the rope for so long before he slips and chokes himself with it. You think you're in control, that you're steering the ship. Then the ship goes under and you're drowning in your own mess.

I should've never let the addiction take root. It wasn't like I woke up one morning and decided to throw everything away. It starts slow, like rust creeping across metal. First a drink here, a joint there, a pill just to quiet the screaming inside. Ana would try to talk to me, those nights when I'd come home too drunk to stand. She'd pull me close and tell me she loved me, that she didn't want to see me destroy myself. And I'd tell her I was fine, that I didn't need her pity, that I was strong. Strong enough to fight it. But I wasn't strong enough for the thing gnawing away at me. It wasn't a monster you could shoot or stab—it was inside, crawling through your veins like poison.

I think about it now, when I'm wide awake at 3 a.m., the memory of her face just out of reach. Her eyes, the way they would soften whenever she saw me—like she was trying to hold onto a version of me that didn't exist anymore. I was already dead in the places that mattered. I didn't know it yet. Or maybe I did. And I didn't care.

There's a moment you realize the drugs are more important than the people around you. It happens when you're so far gone that you can't remember the last time you ate, or slept, or even bothered to look in the mirror. All you care about is the next hit. You're not a person anymore—you're a hole, just sucking in whatever it can to fill itself. Ana didn't sign up for that. But she didn't walk away right away. She stayed. She stayed longer than anyone should've.

It was the last time I saw her that sticks. I was on the couch, passed out, shaking. I hadn't eaten in two days, and I barely had enough energy to lift my head. But she was there, looking down at me, trying to make sense of what we were. She didn't get mad—she wasn't the kind of person who could yell and scream. She just... broke. She said, "I can't do this anymore. I can't keep watching you kill yourself."

And I wanted to scream at her, tell her it was my choice. But the words wouldn't come out. I wanted to say something smart, something that made it her fault. But all that came out was a shitty, self-pitying chuckle. She looked at me, just for a second, like she saw the man I used to be. Then she closed the door behind her, and that was it.

The next few weeks were a blur. I think I tried to call her once, or maybe twice, but I just couldn't find the strength to even dial the number. What was the point? She didn't need me anymore. I was just a fucking ghost, a fucking junkie, and she was better off without me.

That's how it happens. You lie to yourself until you believe the lies. You tell yourself that you're the one who fucked it all up, that you're the one who never really deserved it. But the truth? The truth is you were never strong enough to keep the ship afloat. You were always waiting for someone else to save you, and when they didn't, you blamed them for not being strong enough to carry you.

But it wasn't Ana who left. It was me. I left her long before she walked out that door. I was already gone—lost to the hunger, the endless thirst that would never be quenched. I tried to fill the hole with pills, with booze, with whatever I could get my hands on, but it never worked. You can drown yourself in the stuff, but it just keeps coming back.

I think that's the real kicker. The shit that's inside you never goes away. It waits. It waits for you to run out of excuses. And then, when you're not looking, it crawls out from the cracks in your skull and it reminds you that you're a piece of shit.

And I can't tell you how many times I've tried to blame the world for this. It's so easy to say it's the system, the fucking city, the way the whole goddamn world just spits you out and leaves you to rot in the streets. That's what they want from you—they want you to believe that you're not worth anything, that you'll never be anything. And it's true, maybe. But at least I had her. I had someone who saw something in me, who saw the part of me that was still trying. But I destroyed that. I destroyed her. All by myself.

The funny thing is, I still blame her. Not directly, of course. But I blame her for giving me hope, for making me believe I could be more than this. I was fine before I met her. I was numb. I wasn't pretending. She gave me the idea that I could do something with my life. But I didn't want it. I didn't want anything more than the fucking drink, the high, the stupid, numbing escape from reality.

Now I'm here, wandering these streets, picking at the scraps of what's left of me. I can't even remember the last time I ate a real meal. I haven't seen her face in years. But it's there, haunting me, every time I close my eyes. She's gone now, probably off with some guy who knows how to treat her right. Good for her, I guess. But the truth is, I'm still here, looking for a way out, but I don't know how to leave.

The Moment Ana Left

I don't know how you can love someone so much and then lose them. It's not like you get to choose when it happens. It just happens, like the world shifting under your feet. One minute, you're walking, you're holding her hand, you're thinking the future's something you're both building together. The next minute, the floor's gone and you're falling, and you don't even have time to scream before you hit rock bottom. But rock bottom isn't a place. It's a feeling.

I remember the day Ana left. I remember her standing in the doorway, looking back at me for the last time. She didn't say a word—didn't need to. There's only so much you can say when the love has died, when you've ruined everything with your own goddamn hands.

She stood there, holding the doorframe like she was trying to hold herself together. Like if she let go of the door, she'd fall apart. I knew I should've tried something—grabbed her arm, said something desperate—but I didn't. I didn't even try. I just sat there on the couch, half-drunk, waiting for the sound of her footsteps to fade.

"You can't keep doing this, Dez," she'd said a few days earlier. "I can't do this anymore. I'm not your damn nurse. I'm not your mother. I'm not here to watch you destroy yourself."

I didn't argue with her. What's the point of arguing when you're already dead inside? I didn't have any good answers, didn't have any more excuses. I couldn't even look her in the eyes when she said it. My pride was all that was left, and I wasn't about to give that up, not even for her.

So she left. She didn't need to say goodbye. The door just closed. And that was it.

I watched her walk down the hallway, and I swear to god, I didn't feel anything. Not at first. Just a numbness, like I was watching it happen to someone else. The sharpness of it came later, like a punch to the gut you don't feel until the next day. When the door slammed behind her, it was like the whole fucking world came crashing down with it.

I'd been watching her for a while, before that moment. Watching her slowly fade from me, like smoke slipping through my fingers. I couldn't stop it. I couldn't stop myself from sinking further into whatever hole I'd dug for myself.

What hurt the most wasn't the leaving. It was the finality. The realization that I had nothing left to give. Not to her, not to anyone. Not even to myself.

I could still see her face in my mind—the way she looked at me when she was still trying. I could see the love in her eyes, like she was seeing something in me that I couldn't see in myself. But that was all gone now, wiped out by the nights I spent face-down in a bottle, the endless excuses I gave myself for why I couldn't change. I had become everything she hated, and she hated me for it.

There's no easy way to say this, but I didn't care. Not at that moment. Not when the door closed. I didn't care because I knew, deep down, that I didn't deserve her anymore. I didn't deserve anything. I was just a shell, a wreckage, living in a city that didn't care. Ana had been my tether, my reason to try, to be better. And when she left, that tether snapped.

There's no recovery from that, not really. You can tell yourself you're going to change, but you never do. Not until it's too late. And when she left, it was too late.

I didn't stop drinking. I didn't stop using. I didn't stop any of it. I just kept going, spiraling faster, deeper, until I was lost—until I was nothing. The numbness took over. The ache from her absence became background noise. But it was always there. Every time I opened my eyes, it was there. The weight of what I had lost.

I remember thinking I could fix it. I remember telling myself that if I just found the right high, the right escape, maybe I'd get enough distance from the pain. But the thing is, you can't outrun the truth. You can't outrun yourself. And that's all I had left—myself. And I hated that person. I hated the man I had become.

She was the last piece of something real. She was the only thing that kept me from drowning in the chaos. I thought she would save me, like I thought I could save her. But we were both too broken. Too far gone.

So, she walked away. And I let her go. I didn't chase her. I didn't beg her to stay. I didn't even try to change. Because I was too far gone, and somewhere deep inside, I knew I was already lost. I had already destroyed us.

Maybe she could've forgiven me. Maybe if I'd stopped before I ruined everything, she would've stayed. But that's not the way life works. You don't get to rewrite the past. You don't get second chances when you burn every bridge you've built.

When she closed that door behind her, it wasn't just Ana that left. It was everything. It was the last bit of hope, the last bit of humanity I had left in me. I was just a ghost now, wandering these streets, trying to drown the truth in a bottle.

And I wonder sometimes, as I sit here alone in the dark, whether I could've saved myself. But I know the answer. The answer is no. There was never any saving me. I wasn't built for it. I was built to destroy, to sink into the mess I made and die in it.

The worst part is that I knew it all along.

Chapter 11: Frank's Influence

Frank's Philosophy

The first time Frank told me how to survive, I thought he was messing with me. But there's no humor on the streets. None at all. Not when your stomach's a goddamn black hole and your bones feel like they've been gnawing on themselves for days. Frank didn't joke. He didn't tell me how to survive—he told me how to stop pretending. "You want to eat? You want to live? Then stop pretending you've got a soul left to lose." He looked at me like I was some dumb kid—like I still believed in the idea of a 'soul' or 'morality.' Like I still thought there was something out there worth saving.

I didn't argue. I didn't have it in me to argue.

We moved through the streets like ghosts. Not in the way people think—ghosts aren't just lost souls wandering around. Ghosts are the people you stop seeing. They're the ones who don't get a second look, who slip through the cracks, forgotten, left to rot under the weight of the city. Frank had that kind of ghostliness in him, and he didn't care who saw it. Hell, he wanted people to notice. Not because he gave a damn about their judgment, but because he needed them to know that he was above all that.

I wasn't there yet. Not completely.

"Survival," Frank said, "it's not some noble cause. You don't get points for being decent when your stomach's empty and your hands are shaking. You want to survive? Then stop pretending there's something left in you worth saving."

He made it sound so simple. So goddamn easy. Like peeling skin off an apple. The city had already done it to me. It had taken everything from me—everything except the hunger. The hunger for survival, for meaning, for whatever scraps I could get my hands on.

The first thing he taught me was how to take. Take what you can when you can. Stop asking permission. Don't wait for anyone to give you shit. If you want it, take it. No shame. No guilt.

At first, it felt like a violation. But you know what? After a while, it just felt like nothing. Like I didn't even exist anymore. Frank's philosophy didn't leave room for doubt. You take what you need, and if it hurts someone in the process, so be it. They're just part of the machine. They'll never miss what they never noticed.

We started small. Some chips here, a bottle of whiskey there. I could feel it in my hands—the weight of something that wasn't mine, the thrill of it, the rush. And then I realized that I didn't feel anything anymore. Not really. It was like a hole had opened up in me and everything I took just slipped right in, disappearing without a trace.

But that was the point. To disappear. To stop feeling the weight of the world on you.

Frank was always ahead of me. He wasn't running from anything anymore, not like I was. He'd already killed everything inside him that made him human. All that was left was instinct, and hunger. There was no guilt in Frank's eyes. There was no sorrow. Just a cold, steady hunger that I didn't quite understand.

"Look around," he said one night. "They'll step on you if you let them. They'll take everything you have without even looking at you. They don't care. So don't you dare care about them. You want to survive? Then stop acting like they're better than you."

I didn't know if I believed him. But I sure as hell didn't have any better answers. I'd spent enough time on these streets to know that survival wasn't about being a good person. It wasn't about fighting for the 'right' thing. It was about getting by. It was about taking the scraps, the leftovers, and pretending you didn't see how much you were already dead inside.

One day we hit a small convenience store. I was starting to feel the pull, the need to steal bigger, take more. I picked up a bottle of cheap vodka, felt the smooth glass in my palm like it was an old friend. I didn't even look at the clerk. He was just another nameless face behind the counter. He didn't see me.

But Frank? Frank could see everything. He could see that the world was a game. A brutal game, but a game nonetheless. And if you weren't playing it, you were getting played.

The clerk glanced at me, just a flicker, but I caught it. Something in his eyes, something like recognition. Like he could see me for what I was. But I wasn't some charity case, some broken thing on the corner. I was just a man doing what he had to do. I wasn't the first person to steal, and I wouldn't be the last. I'd made myself a part of this machine.

Frank saw me staring at the clerk. He saw the way I hesitated.

"You're thinking too much," he said, voice flat. "That's your problem. You don't get to think anymore. Not out here. Not on these streets. You either take what you need, or you starve."

And that was it. That was the lesson. No thinking. No morality. No hesitation. You take. You eat. And you keep moving.

By the time we hit the alley, I felt different. The vodka was burning in my stomach, but it didn't feel like I was getting drunk. It felt like I was being erased. Slowly, methodically. Each step I took in Frank's direction was a step further away from the person I used to be.

And every time I used someone, every time I manipulated them, I felt the pieces of me cracking, breaking apart. Frank had told me I needed to stop pretending I had a soul. But I didn't know if I could even remember what one felt like. I didn't know if I had anything left that could be called a soul.

When we were a few blocks down, Frank turned to me, eyes still sharp, still calculating. "You want to survive, Dez? You want to make it out here?" His gaze was steady, unforgiving. "Then stop pretending you have a fucking soul. It's dead. It's all dead. And the sooner you realize that, the better off you'll be."

I felt something then. A twist in my gut. Not guilt. Not yet. But maybe fear. Fear that I was too far gone to come back. Fear that I was already too deep in this to crawl out.

But I didn't stop.

I kept moving.

The Breaking Point

I never really understood how fast you can die inside, how quickly you can become a shell of yourself. One minute, I was still pretending to be human—miserable, sure, but human—and the next, I was on the other side of that line. That line you cross when you stop fighting to hold on to whatever dignity you've got left. And I don't know if it was Frank who did it or if I was just waiting for the excuse.

We're standing outside this corner convenience store, Frank's hand rubbing against the knife in his jacket pocket like he's trying to make sure it's still there. The streetlight above us flickers, like the world's got something to prove, like it wants to be dark and ugly just for the hell of it. Frank's talking—his voice is dry, like the words have been stripped of any humanity.

"You want to live? You want to eat?" he says. He sounds like a man reading a script, no emotion, just the facts. "Then stop pretending you have a soul, Dez. Souls don't fill up with whiskey or candy bars or a warm bed. Souls get you dead. You understand that? You understand you're not here to be a good person? You're here to survive. End of story."

I nod, like I believe him. I want to. Hell, I need to. What choice do I have, really? The world's been taking things from me since I was born, stealing parts of me like it was owed, and I've spent every goddamn day fighting to keep the pieces that are left. But now, I'm starting to wonder if I even *care* about the pieces anymore.

The store is warm inside. It smells like stale coffee, like it's been awake too long. The hum of the refrigerator is too loud, too perfect for a place that should be more alive. Frank walks in first, and I follow because I don't know what else to do. I'm not even scared anymore. Maybe I should've been, but I've lost that feeling. Fear is something for people who think they have something to lose.

Frank goes straight to the counter, his hand still in his jacket. He's got that look on his face like he's not even *there*. He's already checked out. His words fall out like they don't belong to him, like they've been practiced a hundred times: "Give me the cash, and nobody gets hurt."

The clerk looks up at him, eyes wide. There's a tremor in the guy's hands as he reaches for the register. I don't blame him for shaking. I think about what I might've done if I was him—if I still had any decency left. Maybe I would've fought back, or maybe I would've just frozen, like I'm doing right now. Because all I can do is stand here, numb, and watch.

Frank's voice cuts through the silence again, harsh as broken glass. "I said, give me the goddamn cash."

I don't know what's worse—the fact that I'm standing here, letting it happen, or the part of me that's starting to like it. The violence. The power. The *control*. It feels familiar in a sick way. I've been stealing from myself my whole life, and now here I am, finally stealing from the world. It's almost too easy.

I hear the register pop open. Frank grabs the bills and stuffs them into his jacket. The whole thing takes less than a minute, and I'm already wondering if this is it—if this is what I've become. I've crossed a line now. No going back.

We walk out of the store, the door slapping shut behind us. I look at the bags in my hand—the candy, the cheap booze—and I feel something in my chest tighten. Not fear. Not regret. But emptiness. It's the kind of emptiness you don't feel right away. It creeps in like fog, quiet at first, then thickening, until you realize you can't breathe without it.

I thought I'd feel powerful, like I had just taken control of my life. But instead, it's like I've stepped out of myself. My feet are moving, but I'm not really here anymore. I don't know who I am anymore. I've done it—I've crossed that line, and now all I have is a hollow feeling inside me, a gnawing, sickly hole where something should've been. My hands shake as I tear open the candy bar, but the taste in my mouth is metallic, like something I can't spit out.

Frank doesn't say anything. He's already thinking about the next score. "You see?" he says, eyes fixed ahead. "You did it. You survived. You're still breathing."

I don't know if I'm still breathing. It feels like I've stopped.

The End of Innocence

I sit back against the concrete, the dirt and piss soaking into my jeans, and I try to breathe. But the air is thick now, suffocating, like the whole city is in on it. The noise—sirens, car horns, the screech of tires on asphalt—becomes a tidal wave, crashing over my head, pulling me under. I don't know how long I've been here, but the cold is already seeping through my bones, gnawing at my skin like a hundred hungry rats.

I try to pull a cigarette from the pack I stole earlier, but my fingers are shaking too much to light it. The match fizzles out on the first strike. Fuck. I try again, but this time I just sit there, the smoke floating in front of my face like a ghost. Everything is quiet inside my head. Too quiet. I don't know where the thoughts go when they die, but I know they've gone somewhere.

There's no escaping it. I can feel it in my gut, the gnawing emptiness that starts to spread from my chest, down into my stomach. It feels like a hole, but it's not a hole. It's more like a weight, pressing down on me. I don't know how to shake it. I don't know how to get away from this feeling, like something inside of me just *died* and I'm left here, holding the corpse. It's not the kind of death you get with a bullet or a knife; it's the slow kind, the kind that comes when you've crossed a line, when you've gone too far.

I think about the store. I think about the clerk's face, eyes wide, mouth trembling, his hands shaking as he counted the cash. Frank's words—*"You survived. You're still breathing."* It's supposed to mean something, right? It's supposed to make me feel... what? Proud? Relieved? It doesn't. It just feels like more weight, more chains. The kind of weight you don't see until you try to move.

I used to think I was different. I used to think I had some kind of grace, some small shred of *decency* left, something that made me better than the people I saw on the streets every day. They'd steal, they'd lie, they'd rob people blind, but *I*... I always thought there was more to it, more than just surviving. I had Ana, and I thought I could get out of this shit. I thought I could build something, even if it was just the illusion of it. I thought I was better than this.

But now I'm not so sure.

I'm not even sure who I am anymore.

Frank's out there, somewhere. Maybe still high off the robbery, still walking around with that empty swagger, like he's king of the fucking world. But me? I can't even look at myself in the reflection of a store window without feeling sick. I used to have a face. I used to have a name. *Dez.* It was a name I could say out loud and think, *I'm somebody.* Now, that name feels like a joke. A punchline nobody ever got.

It's not just the robbery. It's everything. The streets. The cold. The hunger. The endless waiting for something to change, and then the bitter realization that nothing ever will. The city's just a giant trap, and we're all stuck in it, chasing scraps while the rich fuckers upstairs are too busy to even notice. They don't care about us. Hell, they don't even see us. And we don't care about them either. The only thing we care about is the next meal. The next drink. The next hit. Anything to make the ache go away for just a minute.

I can feel the weight of everything pressing on me now. The cold is biting harder, but it's not the worst part. The worst part is that I don't even care. I used to care about warmth, about the world being a little bit better, but now? Now, it's just the cold, and the noise, and the hunger, and the nothing. I'm nothing.

I don't know what I was expecting, but it wasn't this. I thought I'd feel powerful, like Frank said. I thought I'd feel like I *won*. But no. What I feel is smaller than ever. It's not power. It's just... emptiness. A hollowness I can't fill with stolen booze, or candy bars, or anything else. It's the kind of emptiness that doesn't go away. And that's what you're left with when you rob a man for his dignity: a hollow space where your soul used to be.

I hear someone shouting down the alley. I don't look. I don't care. It's just noise. Just another person in this city, trying to make themselves heard, trying to carve a little bit of meaning into all the shit. But nobody's listening.

A woman stumbles by, eyes glazed, dragging her feet like she's trying to escape from something, or maybe just trying to disappear. She doesn't even look at me, doesn't even *see* me. I could say something to her, but what would I say? *Hey, you wanna share a moment of despair with me? Wanna sit down and talk about how we're all just wasting away in this hellhole?*

I pull my jacket tighter around me, but the cold still gets in. The city's a wound, and I'm just another scar on its skin.

I think about Ana. I think about how we used to talk, about our plans to get out of here, to move to somewhere warmer, somewhere with a future. I remember the way she'd look at me, eyes soft, like she believed in me. But I don't believe in myself anymore. I don't believe in anything. Not in Frank's survivalism, not in Ana, not in a goddamn thing.

The robbery doesn't mean anything now. It doesn't even matter that I survived. What does it mean to survive if you've lost everything that made you human? Frank's right about one thing, at least. There's no soul left in this city, not for the likes of me. I wonder if there ever was.

I hear footsteps, closer now. They stop. Someone's standing there, just out of my line of sight. I don't care to look. Doesn't matter who it is. Another faceless stranger.

"You okay?" they ask.

I don't answer.

The person keeps walking, their footsteps receding into the distance. And I stay there, wrapped in my coat, the bitter cold eating through my skin, wondering if I'll ever be anything more than just another shadow in the dark.

The city closes in around me, and the noise—so loud, so fucking loud—becomes nothing more than a dull hum in the background. It's like it's drowning me. And I'm drowning with it. I think I hear Frank's voice again, faint, echoing in my mind: *"You survived. You're still breathing."*

But I don't feel alive anymore.

I just feel like a thing. A body that keeps moving, keeps surviving, but is already long dead.

Chapter 12: The City's Indifference

The Invisible Man

The city hums in a rhythm I can't keep up with. I walk through it, a ghost, invisible, part of the pulse but not a part of the heartbeat. The sidewalks are a battleground of hurried steps, eyes glued to phones, faces buried in thoughts that have nothing to do with me. I'm nothing to them. Not even a bump in the day. The rich folk speed by in their shiny suits, their perfume choking the air, while the tourists shuffle along, pretending to be thrilled to be here, snapping pictures like there's something worth capturing. They don't even see me, don't even care enough to stare.

My boots slap the wet concrete as I shuffle through the mess, the din of the crowd like a constant buzz in my ears, a low hum I can't escape. The city is a machine, and I'm just another cog. Just another guy wandering these streets, blending into the concrete jungle like a scrap of paper in the wind. I wonder how many others are like me, stuck in this human meat grinder, scraping by, wondering when the damn thing will finally chew us up.

I take a corner by the old coffee shop on Broadway. The neon sign flickers in the rain, casting a sickly red glow over the slush-filled sidewalk. I pass a woman huddled under a ratty blanket by the door, her fingers twitching in her sleep, maybe dreaming of a life she once had or a life she could have. I don't know. I don't care. She's just another fixture on the street. I could be her. She could be me. Who knows? Who gives a shit?

I feel the weight of the city on my chest, the sharp, biting cold that cuts through my coat like a knife. My hands are numb, but that's nothing new. The cold's a friend. It keeps you alive. It keeps you aware. It makes you feel something when everything else feels like a void. But it also makes you feel small. Weak. Powerless. The city doesn't care if you're cold. Doesn't care if you freeze on its doorstep, or if you starve to death in its belly. It's indifferent. No one stops. No one gives a damn.

I pass a guy selling hot dogs on the corner. His cart's steaming, but the smell doesn't do anything for me anymore. I don't want the food. I don't want the company. What do I want? I don't even know. I just keep moving, keep walking, because that's all I can do. Move. Maybe the city will forget me if I stop.

I stop anyway. I find a bench in some park, the one by the library. It's empty. The rain's tapering off, leaving puddles that reflect the city's lights in sickly colors. I sit down, feeling the cold metal seep through my jeans. My stomach growls, but the hunger feels like an afterthought now. When you're out here long enough, you stop caring about food. You stop caring about a lot of things. Maybe that's what survival is. Just shutting off the parts of you that still feel human.

I light a cigarette, flicking the lighter with fingers that shake. I inhale, the smoke thick in my lungs. I hate it. I love it. It burns, but it's the only burn that's still mine.

I don't even know how I ended up like this. I used to dream about getting out of this—out of the streets, out of the stench, the filth, the stares. But somewhere along the way, those dreams died, one small piece at a time. First it was Ana. Then it was the job. Then the apartment. Then any hope that life could be different. The way things are now is the way they've always been, and it feels like the way they'll always be. A long, gray stretch of nothing.

Frank once told me, "The city doesn't care if you live or die, man. It doesn't even know you exist. It's just a beast chewing its way through the day."

At the time, I thought he was full of shit. I thought there was something left worth fighting for, something in me that mattered. But I'm not so sure anymore. I've seen too much, and I've let too much slide. It's hard to hold on to something when you've been torn apart by this place. The truth is, Frank was right. The city's indifferent. The people are indifferent. I'm invisible. A ghost in a crowd of millions. I walk around, pass by people, and they look through me like I'm not even there. They're too busy, too important, too wrapped up in their own stories to care about mine. I used to think I mattered. Now, I wonder if anyone ever really does.

I watch people walk by, their feet splashing in the puddles. They move fast. They move like they have somewhere to be. I don't know if they're escaping or running toward something. But I don't care. I don't care about anything anymore. I've stopped looking for things that make me feel human. Maybe I gave up too soon. Maybe I was just tired of fighting.

I flick the butt of the cigarette into the puddle, watching it sizzle. It feels like the end of something, like a last attempt to make my mark before it all disappears. It doesn't matter. Nothing does. I can feel myself slipping further and further into the cracks, disappearing into the cracks. I'm not a person anymore. I'm just a body moving through this place, breathing in the air and taking up space, but never really existing.

The rain starts again, a soft drizzle, but it doesn't matter. It doesn't change anything. The city keeps moving, and I keep moving with it, a piece of the puzzle no one bothers to notice.

Encounters with the Public

There are moments when I feel like I'm not even really here. Just a blur in the eyes of the city, drifting through the crowds without being seen. People brush against me, but no one even looks twice. Tourists with their cameras aimed at the Empire State Building, or maybe the Statue of Liberty, have no interest in the human wreckage standing beside them, right there, under their noses. Their eyes gloss over me like I'm part of the landscape—something in the background, irrelevant, like a piece of litter blowing by. I don't exist, not to them.

I'm an invisible man.

I've tried to make them see me. I've asked, "Got a dollar?" or "Spare some change?" but they just keep walking, quickening their pace, as if the very idea of stopping to acknowledge me would slow them down, make their world fall apart. Maybe it would. Maybe that's why they keep moving, eyes fixed forward like they're on a mission to a place that has nothing to do with me.

I'm nothing but a thing in the corner of their vision.

The cold gets to me, seeps into my bones, but I ignore it. I know this city, know its rhythm by now. It's a city of avoidance, of hyper-stimulation and dead eyes. People walk by like they've got the world figured out, like they don't see the real world—the one behind the glass, behind the flash of the next Instagram photo. They're too busy living their little pretend lives to notice that some of us are rotting on the pavement.

I pass a businessman in a suit, his collar starched so stiff it could cut glass. He glances down at me like I'm some kind of stray dog—disgusted, maybe a little wary, but most of all, indifferent. I ask him for a dollar. He sneers, like he's stepping over a dead rat, like my voice didn't even touch him, and he hurries on. It's not the first time I've seen that look. I'm familiar with it now. I'm used to it. It doesn't sting anymore. I don't know if that's worse than the sting. When something stops hurting, it means you've been broken enough times to forget how to feel.

I keep walking, dodging between crowds like I'm a ghost caught in the wind, my footfalls barely registering. The tourists are snapping photos of themselves in front of skyscrapers like they've just stepped into some dream of a perfect life, oblivious to the fact that their happiness is built on a million shattered dreams, scattered across these very streets. I wonder if they'd be happy to see me in one of their pictures, if they'd smile and put me in the frame as a symbol of their generosity. "Look at us, we helped this guy!" What a fucking joke. I'm not part of their picture. I'm just a shadow passing through their fake little worlds. I don't belong to their narrative.

It's when I see the woman walking her dog that the feeling gets worse. She's in her fancy yoga pants, looking like she's just stepped out of a Lululemon ad, and she looks right through me—doesn't even flinch when I step in front of her. She's got a dog with her, a little fluffy thing, the kind that costs more than a month's rent in Queens. The dog looks at me. Not her. Just me. But the woman doesn't see it. She doesn't even know I'm there. She looks past me like I'm a tree or a piece of street furniture.

"Excuse me," I mumble, but she doesn't respond. She just keeps walking, the dog trotting happily beside her. That's how it goes, though, right? They have everything they need. Their dogs are more important than the people who sleep on the sidewalks, and their problems are bigger than ours, even though they're living in some kind of plastic-wrapped fantasy.

I take a seat on a low wall outside the park, the one near the fountain. It's where the pigeons like to hang out. I stare at the water as it spills out in little streams. The sound is comforting in its way—white noise against the chaos. It reminds me of when I was a kid, how I used to dream about a life that wasn't this. Funny how the past can still surprise you with its cruelty. The way I used to feel like I mattered, like I could have a real life. But that's gone now. The city's swallowed it whole, and it doesn't even notice.

I light a cigarette, the flame flickering in the wind, and I pull in the smoke, feel it burn my lungs. That's something, at least. It's real. I don't have much left that's real.

The people pass by, and I watch them. Sometimes I wonder what they think when they see me. Do they feel bad for me? Do they think I deserve this? Do they think I'm a failure? Sometimes I feel like I don't even deserve to be here. Like I'm taking up space that should belong to someone else. Some part of me still believes that maybe, just maybe, there's a place in this city for someone like me. But the rest of me knows better. The rest of me knows that I'm a ghost now, just a leftover piece of humanity that doesn't belong. I'm not even supposed to be here.

I see the cops at the corner of the street, talking to some other homeless guy. They've got that look—the one that says they've seen it all before, that this guy doesn't matter. They don't care if he's hungry, or cold, or if he's just trying to survive. They don't care. They're just doing their job. They'll shuffle him off, tell him to move along, give him some empty words that don't mean shit. I know how it goes. I've seen it a thousand times. It's like being a part of a play you don't remember auditioning for.

A guy walks by with a bag full of groceries, the plastic crinkling as he carries it to his car. I can smell the fried chicken through the bag. It's warm, greasy, delicious. I wonder what it's like to eat something that's not a half-frozen can of soup. I watch him walk away, and I feel my stomach twist. It's not hunger anymore. It's anger. The city doesn't care if you eat, if you sleep, if you live or die. It just keeps moving, and you have to keep moving with it or you get left behind.

But the worst part is, the hardest part, is that I'm not just a ghost in the city—I'm a ghost in my own life. I used to be someone else. I used to think I could matter. But that guy is long gone now. I've been forgotten by everyone, including myself.

I flick the cigarette butt into the fountain and watch it float away, just another piece of trash, lost in the current.

A Brief Moment of Clarity

I'm sitting on a bench in the park, watching the people walk by, their faces floating like ghosts in the air. It's the kind of park where families go to pretend the world isn't falling apart. Children running in circles, their laughter bouncing off the trees. Parents smiling, proud of their little victories in a world that never gives a damn. And me? I'm just the guy they avoid. The guy they pretend doesn't exist. I'm invisible, like some half-dead soul that nobody notices, not even long enough to spit on.

I can't remember the last time someone looked at me—really looked at me. Not with pity, not with disgust, but just saw me. Saw this broken body sitting on this bench, staring at the world like it's got something to offer. But it doesn't. The world's just a carnival ride for the lucky, a slow-motion car crash for the rest of us. And here I am, stuck at the intersection, watching people pass by with their heads held high, pretending they've got it all figured out.

I watch a family walk by. The kid's laughing, the mother's smiling, the father holding a soda, not a care in the world. And I realize—right there, like a punch to the gut—that for them, the world is still a place of innocence. They've got a future, a place to go, people to love them, places to sleep. The sun breaks through the clouds just then, and for a moment, it's like everything in this goddamn city could still make sense. It's a brief moment, like the sun's shining just for me—like I'm not invisible, not dead yet, just hanging by a thread.

But then it fades. The sun's gone, the world's spinning again, and I'm stuck here, stuck with this feeling. This realization that I'm already dead. Not physically, not yet. But everything that mattered is gone. Every shred of hope, every dream, every goddamn plan to make something of myself—that's dead. I'm just waiting for my body to catch up.

This isn't a city for people like me. Hell, this isn't a city for anyone who's ever felt real. If you're not part of the hustle, the show, the one-way ticket to the top, then you're just another ghost wandering around, waiting for the right moment to disappear. And people know it. They know it, but they don't care. They don't even want to look.

I think about the woman who walked past me earlier. The one with the dog. She looked right through me, like I was a bench or a lamppost or a piece of trash. A non-entity. Nothing worth acknowledging. I asked her for some spare change, and she didn't even flinch. Just kept walking, like I wasn't even there. Like I didn't exist. And you know what? She's got every right. Why should she see me? She's too busy with her dog, with her life, with her fucking lattes and whatever else keeps her up at night. She'll never know what it's like to wake up and realize you're just another face in the crowd—except you're not even part of the crowd. You're the guy they step over, the one they avoid like the plague.

It's not even about money. I don't need her change. I need her to look at me. To really see me. But I won't ask again. I don't want her charity. I don't want her pity. I just want to feel something other than this fucking emptiness gnawing at my insides.

I close my eyes, feel the cool breeze hit my face. It feels good. For a second, I can almost pretend everything's normal. Almost. But then the car alarms start, and the smell of hot dogs wafts by, mixing with the smell of piss and sweat. And it's like I'm dragged back to reality.

I can't even remember the last time I had a decent meal. A real meal, not some garbage from a half-closed diner or a hot dog cart where the vendor's too busy to care. I used to eat like I had a future. Like I had a fucking shot at something more. But now? Now I just eat because it's something to do. Just something to fill this hole. Like the bottle, like the cigarette, like the bed I sleep in when I can find a cardboard box that's not too wet. There's no luxury. Just survival. And if you're lucky enough to survive, well, that's the win. No one ever tells you that, but it's the only truth worth knowing.

A man walks by in a suit. He's got his head down, eyes glued to his phone, his face set in the kind of expression that says "I'm better than you." I know that look. I've seen it a thousand times. He probably doesn't even know what a homeless man looks like anymore. He's too busy climbing whatever corporate ladder he's stuck on. His world's clean, neat, shiny. Mine's dirty, real, and rotting at the edges.

I wonder if he's happy. Probably not. Probably got the same void inside him I've got. But he's too busy to feel it. Too busy with his meetings, his deals, his plans to care. I'm not so lucky. I've got nothing but time to think about it. Time to sit here and wait for a city to forget I'm alive.

Somebody else walks past me, this time a tourist. She's snapping pictures of the buildings, of the big billboards, of the fucking skyline. She doesn't even notice me sitting here, rotting in her peripheral vision. I should hate them, the tourists. But I don't. They're just as much part of the show as anyone else. They're just playing their part in the big illusion. They don't see me because they're too busy looking at the buildings. The lights. The glitz. The glamour. But not the people. Not the people who actually live here. They don't want to see us.

I feel a sudden, sharp pain in my chest. It's a familiar sensation—this thing that aches and spreads like fire through my veins. A sudden, deep longing for something I can't even put a name to. I want to scream. I want to break something. But I don't. I just sit here, staring at the sky, watching the clouds drift away as though nothing in this world matters. It doesn't.

And yet, for the briefest of moments, I feel something—a flicker of life, of longing, of... possibility. It hits me like a freight train, and for a second, I'm caught between wanting to run and wanting to stay in this park and let the world pass me by, let it swallow me whole. But I can't move. I'm stuck in this moment, this frozen instant of clarity. Like a man on the verge of drowning, gasping for air, knowing that the surface is just out of reach.

But the moment's gone. The pain's still there, like a dull ache in the back of my throat, but it's fading. Just like everything else.

I could get up, I could walk away. But where would I go? What's the point of walking anywhere when you've already walked through every possible door and found nothing but empty rooms? What's the point of staying alive when all you're doing is waiting for the inevitable?

But even so, I'm still here. Still waiting. Still breathing.

And for now, that's all I can do.

Chapter 13: Ana Returns

The Accidental Meeting

I'm sitting on the curb, my back pressed against the brick of some overpaid condo, watching the people rush by like they have somewhere to go. I don't. And I don't care. I haven't cared in years.

I can hear the murmurs of city life, the honk of horns, the squeal of subway tracks, and for a second, it's all just noise—like everything I've ever done, everything I've ever been, is just noise.

And then I see her.

Ana.

She doesn't see me. Not at first. She's walking with some polished prick in a suit, probably talking about his stocks or whatever it is that makes men like him so fucking important. They pass by, their shoes clicking on the sidewalk like they're marching toward some dream that'll never happen. I watch her—her face, the way she holds herself now. She's all clean and put together, but something in her eyes, it's like the same Ana from before, the girl I used to know. The one who didn't mind the dirt under her nails, the one who didn't mind me being filthy and drunk and lost.

But that's gone now, isn't it? She's with him, and I'm just a fucking ghost. A silhouette in the background of their perfect little life.

Her husband—if that's even who he is—doesn't notice me. They're too busy with each other, too busy with the life they've built while I've spent the last few years fucking mine up.

But Ana. She stops. Her heels dragging on the pavement, the second it registers—her eyes flicker to me, and I see it. The shock. The recognition. Her hand tightens around the strap of her purse like I'm some kind of predator waiting to pounce.

For a second, there's nothing. The city stops moving. The people are just shadows around us. And it's just Ana and me. Just us, the way it used to be, only we're not who we used to be.

Her lips part, but she doesn't say anything. She just stares at me like she can't figure out if I'm real or if I'm some ghost from her past.

I don't say her name. It's not worth it.

She's with him now, the shiny man, the guy who probably wipes his ass with hundred-dollar bills. There's no place for me in her world anymore. She can't afford me. She's made it clear enough over the years. That last time I called her, she told me she didn't have time for people like me. People who ruined their lives. People who got stuck in the cracks of society like rats scurrying underfoot.

And now, here we are. Years later. And she's still the same. But I'm not.

I'm worse.

She's got this look in her eyes—a mix of pity and guilt—but she pulls herself together fast. She's good at that, always has been. She gives me one last glance, like she's trying to remember if I was ever anything more than a mistake, and then turns her back on me.

Her husband doesn't even notice. He's probably thinking about his fucking golf game or how much better he is than everyone else.

It's funny how people change, isn't it? I used to be the guy who could make her laugh, make her smile. The guy she could fuck in the back of a cab or on a park bench and not care who saw. And now? I'm the guy she can't even acknowledge in public.

I turn away from them, but it doesn't matter. It's all the same. She's gone, the woman I once knew, and now there's only this—the leftover ghost of what could've been. The stupid shit I did, the mistakes I can't undo.

I look down at my hands—dirty, cracked, raw from years of living in places where people pretend they don't exist. I close my eyes for a moment, trying to escape the images of Ana's face—her husband's smug grin—and then I remember something.

I was alive once. Not this. Not the ghost I am now, but a person with hope, with dreams. But those are gone. So, what's left?

Nothing. Nothing but the hollow feeling in my chest, like I've been slowly drained of everything that ever mattered.

I can still feel her eyes on me, though, just for that one moment, before she turned away.

The fucking bastard. He's taking her to some fancy dinner, probably to talk about the next house they're going to buy, while I sit here like some fucking nobody. A roach in the corner of a room they'll never even notice.

I smile bitterly. "Yeah, that's right. Go on. Don't look back."

And just like that, she's gone.

The world keeps moving.

And I stay the same.

Regret and Reconciliation

I never expected to see her again. I don't expect much these days. Not after the world's done its best to bury me in its rubble. But there she was—Ana—walking past me like I wasn't a part of her past, like she hadn't once been the only thing I cared about.

I was sitting on the corner, my back pressed against the brick of some store that's been shut for years. The smell of piss, cheap coffee, and rot thick in the air, and me, just another stain on the city's sidewalk. My stomach growled like it always does, a reminder of my place in all of this. But then, out of nowhere, she walks by, her heels clicking on the pavement in that rhythm I used to know by heart. Clean. Polished. She was a different woman now.

I watched her walk, saw the way she carried herself, all the grace she never had when we were together. I used to think we'd make it, that she and I were two halves of some kind of beautiful thing. But now, she was just a ghost of that woman, a woman who moved in a world I didn't belong in anymore. She didn't even look at me at first.

But I knew her.

She didn't know me, not anymore. Maybe she'd buried me so deep in her mind I was just a faint blur now, something she had to scrub out when she remembered it. But I could still see her. I could see the way she pulled her coat tighter, how her jaw clenched when she noticed me—just a little twitch of her face, the way a person does when they realize they've stepped into their own grave. That moment, that split second when she froze, I could feel her eyes burning into me like she was trying to make me disappear. She wasn't strong enough to look away completely.

She turned her head, and for a second, I thought she might say something. Ask how I was doing. Ask what the hell happened to me. But she didn't. She just stared, that quick flash of recognition—then it was gone, replaced by something colder. It was the same look people give when they see a dead thing on the street and just step over it.

Her husband, some well-dressed asshole I'd never seen before, didn't even notice. He kept walking, arm wrapped around her like a security blanket. Like she was his, like she'd always been his.

I wanted to scream. I wanted to shout her name, demand some kind of answer for this, for the way she just walked away without even sparing me a second. But the words wouldn't come.

I sat there in the silence, a part of me dying with each step she took further away. She didn't need to say anything. She didn't have to say anything. Her back was all the answer I needed.

I didn't move. I didn't chase her down. I just stayed there, letting her walk into the life I couldn't be a part of anymore. That life wasn't for me. I wasn't built for that kind of life. I'm not built for anything, really.

And that's when it hit me. I wasn't dead yet, but I was already gone.

I'd spent so many years chasing ghosts, trying to find something I'd lost in some stupid, empty search for meaning. For a while, I thought I could change. Thought I could get it all back. But that's a lie, isn't it? Nothing comes back. Not when it's lost like that. I could feel the truth of it now, pounding through my skull like a bad drumbeat. She was gone. She was never coming back. She'd found her life, and I was just something that didn't fit anymore. Something she'd buried.

I could taste the bitterness in my mouth, that metallic aftertaste of regret, sour and sharp. I replayed it over and over in my head—the way she stopped, the way her face twisted in recognition, the way she couldn't quite hide her disappointment in me. But I didn't want to relive it. I didn't want to care.

The worst part is that I can't stop thinking about it. About her, about what could have been. I thought maybe, somehow, I'd find a way to fix it. Maybe, if I had the right words, the right kind of apology, she'd take me back. But there's no fixing this. No apology big enough to turn this into something that doesn't taste like ash in my mouth.

She wasn't mine anymore.

I thought I could fix it. But I couldn't. Not then. Not now.

And there's nothing left to say. I've been sitting here for hours now, stuck in this mess of thoughts, watching the world spin around me, and I can't even figure out why I'm still here. I keep telling myself I'll make something of this life. That one day, I'll pull myself out of this shit. But that's just a lie too.

You can't climb out of the gutter if the whole damn world's against you.

She doesn't need me. Hell, she never did. She's fine without me. She's got a man now who can give her everything I couldn't. I'm nothing but a shadow, an afterthought. She doesn't look back because there's no reason to.

I thought I had a chance. I thought I could change. But I can't. She's gone. I'm stuck.

The funny thing is, I'm still alive. And that's the only thing that keeps me awake at night—the fact that I'm still breathing, still here, dragging myself through each day like it means something. But I know it doesn't. I know I'm already dead.

The city doesn't care.

I can't find a way out of this.

And I can't let go of her.

I keep seeing her face, every time I close my eyes, that moment when she looked at me and then turned away. Like I wasn't even real. Like I never mattered.

And maybe I didn't.

But I'm still here, aren't I?

Final Goodbye

I watch Ana disappear into the crowd, like a flame snuffed out too quickly. One second, there—burning bright—and the next, swallowed by the concrete jaws of the city. She's gone. Just like that. No tearful goodbyes. No last-minute rescue. She doesn't look back. She doesn't need to. She's got everything she ever wanted. And I've got nothing.

A part of me expects it to feel like a punch to the gut, like I should be staggering under the weight of it, but the truth is, I don't feel anything but a cold, quiet emptiness. I'd been preparing for this for years, only now it's finally here. Her life is better without me. I know it. Hell, we both knew it then, but she stayed anyway, waiting for something that was never going to change. She loved me, once, but love doesn't keep the lights on when the world goes dark. And mine had long since gone out.

She didn't even hesitate. The moment she recognized me, there was that flicker of something—shock, pity, sadness, maybe a little fear. And then it was gone. It was like she'd seen a ghost—faded and forgotten. I wasn't a man anymore. I was a memory she couldn't erase fast enough. I can't blame her. I couldn't stand the person I've become either. I used to be someone who had a future. I used to have hope, and dreams. I used to believe in something.

Now, I'm nothing. Just this hollow shell of a man stumbling through the streets like a stray dog sniffing at scraps. But that's all I am. Scraps.

I crush the last of my cigarette into the filthy sidewalk. The ember hisses, but it doesn't burn long enough to hurt. Nothing does anymore. I can't remember the last time I felt something real. I'm tired, bone-tired, of this endless cycle—of existing just to exist. I can feel the weight of my own skin. I feel my hands trembling, like my own body is betraying me.

The people pass by me, too busy with their own lives to give a shit about mine. It's funny, isn't it? How easy it is to become invisible in a world that thrives on ignoring the broken. I stand there, frozen in place, as the crowd swirls around me. They don't look at me. They don't see me. They couldn't care less if I drop dead right here on this sidewalk. They've all got their own worlds to attend to. Their own little wars to fight. I don't exist in theirs.

I used to think I was someone special, you know? That I had some kind of spark, some fire inside me that could light up a room. But now, I'm just another nobody. Just another discarded man on the sidewalk, unnoticed. My heart's been broken for years, and I've been walking through the shards without bothering to look down. I keep moving forward. Keep putting one foot in front of the other. It's what you do when you've given up. You keep moving.

But Ana, she—she's moving forward, too. And I'll never catch up to her. Never.

I keep walking, letting the streets swallow me whole. My legs ache, but I don't stop. It's the only thing that makes sense anymore. Keep moving. Because if I stop, if I let myself think about it too much, I'll drown in that regret. The city swallows you whole, but it doesn't even care that you're choking on the way down.

I don't know how long I've been walking. The cold air feels like a razor across my skin. I look up at the skyline, but all I see is emptiness. The lights flicker, distant stars that don't even care if I'm here to watch them burn out. I feel the weight of the city pressing down on me, like I'm suffocating under it.

You want to know what it's like to be invisible? To disappear? Try being homeless in New York. People look through you like you're part of the scenery. They don't see the man behind the grime, the desperation, the brokenness. It's easier for them that way. It's easier for all of us, really. No one wants to see the rot. No one wants to face the truth of how close we all are to falling apart.

I see a couple walking by, their hands intertwined like they're the last two people on earth. The woman's laughing at something the man said, her eyes bright, full of hope. I almost feel something then. Almost. But it's not jealousy. It's just an empty pit opening up in my chest. I used to be that guy. I used to be the one who had a hand to hold, a heart to give. But now, it's just me. Alone. Like I always was.

I take a deep breath, but it doesn't fill my lungs. It's just air, empty and cold. I wonder, sometimes, if I even remember what it feels like to love. Really love someone. To hold them close and not worry about tomorrow. To believe that maybe, just maybe, things could get better. But I've lost that. Somewhere along the way, I lost the part of myself that cared. And the worst part is, I don't even care anymore.

The streets blur together, a series of harsh lights and shadows. I don't know where I'm going. I never did. But I'm not going back. Not to her. Not to any of it. It's too late for that. The man I used to be—he's long gone. There's no place for him in this world anymore.

I stop in front of a corner store. The neon sign buzzes weakly above me. I stare at it for a second, just long enough to wonder if I still have a reflection. Probably not. Probably just another shadow in a world full of them. But I don't care enough to check.

I turn away from the store, from everything, and start walking again. The night stretches on forever, but I keep moving.

Because that's all I can do. Keep walking. Even when there's nothing left to walk to.

Chapter 14: Stevie's Death

The Slow Decline

Watching a man die is a lot like watching a tree rot from the inside out. It's slow. It's ugly. And you don't really see it happening at first. You just wake up one day and realize that the branches aren't bending the same way anymore. That the bark's turned brittle and the leaves aren't coming back.

Stevie's dying. That's what I've figured out. I can't lie to myself anymore. He's not the man he used to be, and maybe that's not the worst thing. Maybe the man he was deserves to die, in a way. But the way it's happening—Jesus Christ—it's not some peaceful slide into death. It's a brutal, ugly thing. And I can't look away, even though I wish I could.

It started a few weeks ago, I think. At first, I just noticed he wasn't around much. He'd come and go like usual, but it wasn't the same. He was slipping out of sight more often. He wasn't showing up for our usual run-ins. Not that we ever hung out much. Stevie was always the kind of guy who kept to himself, drinking, smoking, keeping the world at arm's length. I always figured that was the deal—he didn't want you getting too close. And I respected that.

But then it happened. One day, I found him sitting in the alley where we'd usually meet, his back pressed up against the brick wall like he was trying to keep himself from falling apart. The first thing I noticed was the sweat. His face was pale as hell, beads of it dripping down his forehead, and he was shaking like he'd just crawled out of a burning building.

"You okay?" I asked, but I already knew the answer. You can see it when a guy's sick, really sick. It's in the eyes, the way the light starts to drain out of them. And in his case, it was the body—sagging, hollowing out, like he was already halfway through the process of dying. The hands, trembling like they'd been through a war that nobody could see.

He just nodded, then coughed—hard, raking his throat the way only someone with deep rot in their lungs can. The kind of cough that could make you want to puke. I wanted to reach out, pat him on the back, say something comforting, but that's not what we did. That's not how it works. Not in the gutter.

"I'm fine," he wheezed, but his voice was thin and hoarse, like the air was too thick for him to get through.

"Yeah, sure," I said, but I knew. I wasn't an idiot.

Stevie was dying. It was just a matter of time. I think maybe I'd been waiting for it. It's like watching a train coming down the tracks—you don't know exactly when it's going to hit, but you can feel it coming, slow and steady. You can hear the whistle.

The next time I saw him, it was worse. He didn't even try to stand. He was slumped against the curb, his eyes half-closed, and there was a bottle of vodka in his hand, but it wasn't doing what it used to do. He wasn't drunk. He was just numb. That kind of numbness you can't fix with liquor.

"You're looking like shit," I said, sitting down next to him on the sidewalk. My voice was a little too harsh. I don't know why I said it. Maybe I thought it'd snap him out of whatever was eating at him. Maybe I thought I could make him fight back.

He didn't respond at first, just looked at me with those eyes—those eyes that had always been full of something, full of defiance, like he'd never been afraid to stare down the world. But now they were empty. Hollow. Like someone had pulled the plug out of his soul, and all that was left was an echo.

"I'm dying, Dez," he said after a long pause, his voice thick and wet. "That's what's going on." He said it with such finality, I almost believed him. Like he was doing me a favor by letting me in on it. Like he was releasing me from having to pretend.

"I know," I said. And for once, I didn't lie. I didn't have any smart-ass comment to throw back at him. I didn't have any of the usual bullshit. I just sat there and let the quiet settle in, like it was all we had left.

Stevie coughed again, and this time he didn't even bother to try to cover it. He just let the sound echo out, jagged and rough, rattling through his chest. I watched him, and I knew—I knew what was coming. I could feel it in the air. I could taste it in my own breath.

He took another swig of the vodka, but it didn't have the same bite to it anymore. It didn't seem to matter.

"You ever wonder why we end up like this?" he asked, and I could hear the fatigue in his voice. The bitterness. The resignation.

"Why we end up on the streets?" I asked, though I already knew the answer. We end up on the streets because life wants us there. Life wants us to see what it really is—ugly, raw, unforgiving. It doesn't care about you, your past, or your future. It'll throw you to the curb and keep walking.

He nodded, slowly, his eyes narrowing like he was trying to see something he'd never see again.

"Yeah, that's it, Dez. The streets don't give a shit about anyone. But it's not just the streets, man. It's life. It's people. It's everything. It's... all of it." He coughed again, and this time it sounded like it was coming from deep inside him, like his lungs were trying to escape his body.

I looked away, not wanting him to see the pity that was probably in my eyes. Not that I could have stopped it if I wanted to. He was right. Life didn't give a shit. And neither did I, not anymore.

"You want me to get you something?" I asked. I don't know why. Maybe it was some kind of reflex. Maybe I thought I could fix him. Or maybe I just wanted to believe I could.

He shook his head slowly, almost imperceptibly, and his lips curled into something that might have been a smile if his face hadn't been so twisted with pain.

"No, man," he said. "This is it. There's nothing left."

And that was it. That was the moment. I'd been waiting for him to fight it, to push back, to say something that would make me believe it wasn't all over. But he didn't. He knew it. He was gone already, just waiting for the rest of him to catch up.

I sat there next to him, a cigarette burning between my fingers, and watched him slip further away, little by little, with every breath he didn't take. And I didn't feel sorry for him. Not really. Not like I should have. What I felt was something colder, something more honest. I felt like I was next in line. And that thought, that cold realization, settled into me like a weight I couldn't shake.

Maybe that was the hardest part: knowing it was too late to help, knowing that I was just as lost as he was.

The Moment of Death

The city's pulse has a rhythm to it that doesn't stop for anyone. Not for the rich in their towers, not for the poor in their gutters, not for the desperate in their alleys. It keeps moving, undisturbed, indifferent to the pain of the people stuck in its underbelly. You learn that quickly when you're homeless. You learn that nobody cares, not even a little bit. Especially not when you're a walking disaster, like Stevie.

I found him one night, right there in the street, his body sprawled out like he was too tired to even move a muscle. At first, I thought he was passed out drunk. I mean, he had been drinking himself into a stupor for days. I guess it's how we cope with the reality of this hell. But this was different.

His chest was rising and falling in desperate, jagged gasps, and there was something about his face—twisted in pain, eyes wild with panic, but there was no one there to help him. He was dying.

There was no mistaking it.

And in that moment, as the sounds of traffic roared over the concrete and the lights of taxis flashed by, I realized something: the city didn't care. Not about Stevie, not about me, not about anybody on the streets. People walked past him, their heads down, eyes on the ground. Some of them even stepped over him, like he was just another piece of litter. I watched it all, helpless. The indifference was suffocating.

I knelt down beside him, but I didn't know what to say. What do you say when someone's dying in front of you? You don't offer them comfort, because they don't need comfort—they need air, or a miracle, or maybe just a fucking prayer, but I don't pray anymore. Hell, I haven't prayed in years. I never really believed, even back when I thought I could fix things.

His breathing was getting worse, each one a rasp, like he was choking on the very air itself. It was too much, but I couldn't look away. Part of me wanted to scream for help, but I knew no one would listen. No one ever listens. People like Stevie are invisible to this city. To the world. To me, too, until this moment.

I looked at him, and he looked back at me. His eyes were glassy, unfocused, and yet there was something sharp in them, something that still knew what was happening. I don't think he had any illusions about where this was going. He wasn't asking for help. He wasn't begging for mercy. He wasn't asking for anything. He was just there, in his pain, accepting it as if it were his punishment for existing.

"You're gonna die, Stevie," I said, because the truth was all I had left to offer him. "You know that, right?" My voice sounded distant, even to me. Like I was talking from somewhere far away, removed from the situation, like I wasn't even in the same room.

He coughed, a wet, broken sound that made me wince. The kind of cough that you get when you're drowning on dry land. And he just nodded, like it was nothing new. Like he'd been waiting for this moment for years.

"Yeah, I know," he rasped, voice barely a whisper. "It's just... faster than I thought."

I didn't know what to say to that. What could I say? Life's always faster than you expect, even when you're standing still. Especially when you're standing still, doing nothing, waiting for the world to pass you by.

I stayed there, kneeling next to him, watching as he fought for air, his body shaking with each breath, the city moving on around us. It felt like a nightmare, like I was in one of those goddamn movies where they show you the worst of humanity, the worst of life, and you can't look away even though you know you should. But there's no escape from it. Not for Stevie. Not for me.

The lights flickered overhead, and a siren wailed in the distance, like the city was trying to remind us that we were both just another casualty of its existence. I could hear voices around us, people talking, laughing, living their lives, and it was like they were all in a different world. A world where Stevie didn't exist. A world where people like him didn't get to die in the middle of a sidewalk, unnoticed, uncared for.

I don't know why I didn't leave. Maybe I thought that if I stayed, it would somehow make a difference. That if I just kept watching, maybe I could make this moment mean something. Maybe I could change the ending. But the truth was, I couldn't. None of us can.

Stevie's gasps grew weaker, each one more desperate than the last. His face twisted again, contorted with pain, and his eyes fluttered closed for a second, then snapped open again, wide and full of terror. He couldn't breathe. He couldn't hold on anymore.

I couldn't help him. And I knew that.

"Don't go, man," I said, even though I knew it was pointless. Even though I knew it wasn't up to me, up to any of us. "Just hang on."

But Stevie didn't hang on. He didn't even try to fight it. He was done.

The last breath he took was a shuddering exhale, his body jerking once like it was trying to escape itself, and then... nothing. His chest stopped rising. The air that had been tearing at his lungs just ceased to exist, and for a moment, the world around us fell silent. Like the city itself was holding its breath, waiting to see what would happen next.

I didn't move for a long time after that. I just sat there, staring at him, at the empty shell of the man who had once been my friend. I could feel the cold creeping into my bones, and I knew that this was it. The moment had passed. The world had moved on. And Stevie was gone.

I didn't cry. I don't think I could have if I wanted to. Not for him, not for me. There was no room for tears, no room for any kind of emotion. Only the cold, hard fact that he was dead, and the city didn't care. And neither did I, not really. I didn't care enough to change anything. I didn't care enough to fight for him. I didn't care enough to fight for myself.

I stood up slowly, taking one last look at Stevie's lifeless body, and turned away. The night was still alive with noise, with movement, with people who didn't care about him, about me, about any of us.

I lit a cigarette, took a drag, and walked off into the dark, hoping that one day, I wouldn't have to do this anymore. But knowing that I would.

Reflection and Realization

The thing about death is, it doesn't ask permission. It doesn't care how ready you are, how much you've been through, or how much you've fucked it all up. It comes when it damn well pleases. Stevie was just the latest reminder of that fact.

I'd dragged his body—lifeless, cold, a sack of skin and bones that had once been a man—into a corner, behind a dumpster, where I thought maybe some dignity could remain. The city was indifferent, but at least I could offer him a little space away from the world that had never given a shit about him. Not really. No one cared enough to mourn him, to mark his passing with anything more than a cursory glance or a shrug. So I did the only thing I could do. I laid him down.

There was no ceremony, no ritual, nothing. Just the weight of his body against the asphalt and the memory of a man who had lived in the cracks of society, invisible until his death came and finally took him.

I watched him there for a while, as if by staring at him long enough I could figure out some meaning to all this. I kept waiting for something to change, for the world to stop moving, for a sign that there was something, anything, more to life than this slow erosion of humanity. But nothing happened. The city's noises continued—sirens, traffic, the endless hum of a place that never sleeps. People walked by, stepping around me like I was the one in the way, like I wasn't even there. Just another part of the landscape.

I took a long drag from the cigarette I'd been nursing. The smoke twisted and curled around my head, filling the empty space between me and the world I didn't belong to. There was no relief in the smoke, no escape from the weight of the moment. Stevie's death felt like just another slow death in a long line of slow deaths. This wasn't the first time I'd watched someone die on these streets. And it wouldn't be the last.

You get used to it, you know? You get used to the bodies piling up—some of them literal, others just the same hollow shells of people who gave up long before they physically dropped. And even though you know it's coming, you never get any easier with it. No matter how many times you watch someone die, you never get used to the fact that life just goes on. You don't matter. You never mattered. And eventually, you'll be nothing more than a memory in someone's sad, regretful glance or a nameless face on a missing persons report.

The silence after Stevie died wasn't peaceful. It was suffocating. It filled me up, pressed against my chest, made my bones feel too small for my skin. My fingers were stiff from the cold, but it was the emptiness I couldn't shake, the way everything I'd known about survival—the scraping by, the dodging of punches and insults, the constant fight just to be seen—felt pointless now. What was the point of it all? Why bother with anything if this was the endgame?

I had to wonder—was I any better than Stevie? We were both hanging on by threads. He had just run out of his faster than I would. We were all just waiting for the same thing, just taking our time getting there. Maybe I had a few more years, but in the end, I'd end up the same way. Alone. Forgotten. Dead in some alley or under a bridge. The world wouldn't miss me, just like it wouldn't miss Stevie.

I felt a sick, bitter laugh rise up in my throat. Survival, that's all it was. But survival wasn't living. It wasn't even really existing. It was a waiting game, a slow unraveling of whatever hope or dreams we might've had before we hit rock bottom. The real irony was, none of us knew when we'd hit it. Some of us stayed in free fall for years, like Stevie. Some of us hit it and didn't even know it, just kept bouncing around from one fucked-up situation to the next. But when the ground finally caught us, it caught us hard.

I stood up and walked away from him, away from the corner and the dumpster. There was nothing left for me there. I couldn't bring Stevie back. I couldn't stop time, couldn't stop the world from spinning, couldn't stop the crushing weight of all this meaninglessness from pressing down on me. But I had to keep moving. There was no choice in it. The city was too loud to stop in. Too indifferent to pause.

Walking through the streets, I could feel the eyes on me. It wasn't even about the people looking, it was about the way they looked. Like I was less than human, like I was a thing they had to avoid—something filthy, something to step around. You can see it in their faces, the way they shift when you ask for spare change, like your desperation is contagious. Like poverty and misery are something you can catch. But you can't. You can't catch this. It's already inside you, already in your blood, and no matter how many baths you take or how many jobs you get, you're never gonna wash it out.

The world doesn't care. You're just part of the machinery, a cog in a system that's been grinding down for so long, it doesn't even know how to stop. So you just keep going. You keep existing in the cracks, moving between the cracks, because there's nowhere else to go. There's nothing else. It's all the same.

As I walked, I could feel the familiar weight of the pavement under my shoes, the way the streets vibrated with the pulse of a thousand indifferent lives. I lit another cigarette, watching the smoke curl up into the dark sky, wondering if this was it. Was this what it was all for? For the cigarette, for the small escape it offered, for the momentary lapse in awareness that the world around you didn't care? It wasn't enough. It never was.

But what else is there? What else can you do when you've been forgotten by the world? When your name doesn't matter and your face is just another blur in the crowd?

Stevie was dead. And one day, I'd be dead too. And that thought, that brutal, cold certainty, seemed to wrap itself around me like the city's breath.

I didn't have the answers. Hell, I didn't even have the questions anymore. But I knew one thing for sure—survival wasn't enough. None of this was enough. It was all just a slow death. A wait. And there was no escaping it. Maybe that's the only truth you can count on in this life—the one thing that's inevitable.

And so I walked. Because that's all I could do. Walk.

Chapter 15: New York as a Living Entity

The City's Cold Embrace

The city's alive. It pulses. You can feel it if you know where to look. Beneath the neon lights, behind the shiny glass, in the shadows where the rats and the lost souls lurk. It's massive, unforgiving, an organism that consumes anything that dares fall through its cracks. I'm part of it now—just another useless cog, grinding away in its indifferent gears.

New York doesn't need me. Doesn't need anyone. People come, people go, like dust, scattered in the wind. And the city? It doesn't even flinch. It just keeps moving, eats up the ones who fall behind, and keeps going like nothing happened. A hundred million bodies, all caught up in the same sick dance, moving to a rhythm that doesn't care if you're alive or dead.

The streets are an open mouth, and it swallows everything—dreams, bodies, hope. I sit here, in the dark alley between two dumpsters, watching the flow of bodies. Tourists with their goddamn selfie sticks, businessmen with their shiny shoes, the occasional junkie with wild eyes. All of them are running, chasing something, but none of them see the truth: the city doesn't care. The city's a machine, and you're just fuel.

Used to be I thought I could escape it. Thought I could be something. Thought I could carve out a space of my own, away from the noise. But that was a joke. The truth is, survival here isn't about living; it's about staying out of the way. If you're lucky, the city doesn't notice you. If you're unlucky, it grinds you to dust.

That's all we are—dust. We float through the cracks of this city, insignificant. People like me, the ones you don't notice, the ones who sleep on sidewalks and beg for change, we're just whispers in the wind. The city doesn't care about us. We're not even worth the trash can. It chews us up, spits us out, and keeps going.

The tourists? They're fools. They see the lights, the skyscrapers, the postcards, and they think they've found paradise. They don't see the dark corners, the hidden parts of the city—the places where people fall through, where they get stuck. They walk around like they're walking through some fairy tale, not realizing that the city isn't interested in their dreams. It's only interested in what it can take.

And the people who make it here? They're just as lost. They don't know any better. They think if they can just get to the top, if they can just hit that magic number, then maybe, just maybe, the city will care. But it won't. The city doesn't care about you. You're a cog, just like the rest of us.

I've seen it all—the suits, the tourists, the businessmen, the hustlers, the addicts. All of them moving, all of them feeding the machine. It doesn't matter who you are. It doesn't matter if you're rich or poor. You'll end up the same. You'll end up dust, swallowed by the beast.

And I'm no different. I've got my spot, my corner, my little piece of New York where I fade into the background, barely noticed. I beg for change, I drink my vodka, I pull the same rags over me at night, hoping I'll get a few hours of sleep before the city decides it's time for me to move again. And I know, deep down, that I'm not going anywhere. This is it. This is all I am now—just another piece of garbage that the city chews up and spits out.

I sit here, in the dirt, watching the world pass by. The city keeps moving, its heart beating without a care for anyone or anything. People come, they go. They walk past me without a glance. I could be dead, lying here in the street, and it wouldn't matter. No one would stop. No one would even blink.

I can feel it in my bones. The city doesn't care. It's not a place for dreams or hope. It's a place for survival. But even survival doesn't mean anything. It's just another form of death. You keep breathing, keep walking, because there's nothing else to do. But you're already dead, aren't you? Just waiting for your turn to be swallowed by the machine.

It's not that I don't understand it. I do. The city is a beast, and we're all its food. But I can't help but feel like there's something wrong with this. Like something deeper's at play here. The city eats everything it can, and then it just keeps going. People, broken and forgotten, fall by the wayside, and no one notices. No one cares.

And yet, I can't stop moving. Even if I wanted to, I couldn't. I'm part of the machine, just like everyone else. I walk because I have no other choice. The city's rhythm is my rhythm, even if it doesn't give a damn about me.

The Absurdity of Existence

There's a way the city chews you up and spits you out without a second thought, and you become part of it—just another scrap in its never-ending cycle. The pigeons know it. The people who sit on park benches pretending to read newspapers know it. And the businessmen in their shiny suits and tie-knots tight as nooses, they know it too. But nobody talks about it. You can't. If you do, you get labeled. Crazy, delusional, lazy. They're all too busy hustling to ask if it's worth it.

I'm sitting on a bench now, just another broken thing in the stream of life, watching the birds fight over crumbs. There's something about them, the way they hop around, hungry, always moving but never really getting anywhere. I guess they're like me. They circle, searching for anything to sustain them, but the city keeps tossing out stale leftovers—never anything real. Not for us. Never for us.

I think about it for a while—the absurdity of it all. All of us just pretending, scrambling, fighting for whatever scraps we can snatch from the jaws of this city. But it doesn't care. You can starve. You can freeze to death on a street corner, and the world will just keep moving. Nobody will even notice. Not unless you're something. Not unless you're famous or rich or important in some way. And you know what? That's the real joke.

People look at me and see a homeless man. A throwaway. Maybe they think I've got problems—mental illness, addiction, maybe both. But they don't see the truth. The truth is, I'm just a cog in the machine, a rat in the maze, a pigeon in the park, fighting for the crumbs that fall off the table. And the machine doesn't care. It doesn't need me. I could die tomorrow, and it would shrug its shoulders and keep on running.

The city moves without pause, its breath like the rumbling of subway trains. It inhales and exhales through the cracks in the pavement, through the filthy gutters. I've gotten used to it—this rhythm of destruction. This indifferent noise. But sometimes it's hard not to feel small in the face of it all. Like I'm nothing. Just another blip in the timeline of a place that doesn't even know I exist.

I'm not even sure when I became invisible. But here I am. People walk by without a glance. I'm used to it. You learn to fade into the background after a while. The city teaches you that. It teaches you that nothing you do matters. It teaches you that nothing you are matters. You're not even a person; you're a part of the machinery that gets ignored, scraped off, thrown away when you're done.

I look at the pigeons again. They're scavenging, fighting over a half-eaten sandwich that some tourist discarded. Their wings flap like broken dreams, desperate to find something, anything, to eat. It's like the whole damn city's in a race to consume everything and everyone, and then it spits them back out—dismantled, unrecognizable. I don't know what's worse: being eaten alive or being forgotten altogether.

And then I wonder: does it matter? Does any of it matter? I used to care about answers. I used to hope that one day I'd find some meaning in all of this—some purpose. Maybe I'd catch a break. Maybe someone would notice me, throw me a bone, tell me I was worth something. But the city doesn't care about you, and life doesn't come with any guarantees.

Survival. That's what it's about. That's all there is. Survive today, survive tomorrow, and just keep your head down until you get hit by a car or freeze to death in your sleep. It's like living in a dream that you can never wake up from. You keep pushing, because what else is there to do? You try not to think too much about the future, because the future doesn't exist. There's only now. Only this moment, and even this moment is already slipping away.

There's a quiet bitterness in me. I try to shake it off, but it clings to me like the cold. It's in the way my legs ache from sitting too long, the way my stomach growls from hunger, the way the city's noise presses in on me, trying to drown me out. But I can't escape it. None of us can. We're all part of the system, feeding the machine, and in return, it spits us out when we're done. It's a cruel, cyclical existence.

I've tried to care. I've tried to convince myself that I could change, that I could be more than just another scrap of humanity crushed beneath the weight of this city. But the truth is, I'm too tired now. Maybe I was never meant for more than this. Maybe we're all just born to disappear. I think about Stevie, how he was gone in an instant. He didn't even make a dent in this world, and neither will I. Neither will anyone else.

I watch the pigeons fly off. There's no more bread for them to fight over, and they take off into the sky like the nothingness they came from. And for a moment, I feel a strange peace, like maybe I'm just like them, a scrap floating in the wind. Maybe I'll never find anything more. Maybe that's the whole point of it all. To disappear into the noise and let the city swallow you whole, without a sound, without a fight.

But then the sirens scream. The voices start up again. And I realize that I'm still here, still breathing, still waiting for something that will never come. And the city keeps moving, oblivious to everything I've just thought.

Maybe it's time to go somewhere else, to another bench or a different corner, just to keep moving with the rest of them. Or maybe I'll just sit here until the cold becomes too much to bear. Either way, nothing changes. Nothing ever changes. And that's the way it's supposed to be.

Acceptance

I've stopped thinking about what happens next. The city has whittled me down to something soft—something that no longer feels the sting of hunger or the burn of need. I've learned how to breathe in this air, thick with exhaust and something darker, a kind of quiet desperation that sticks to your skin like sweat. I don't fight it anymore. I let it settle. Let it numb me.

The hunger's a distant hum in the back of my throat now. It used to claw at me, sharp and insistent. But now it just fades in and out like the trains, like the sirens. A sound that comes and goes, part of the rhythm. The world keeps moving, but I'm not moved by it. I've learned to sit still. To let it pass through me, like I'm part of the furniture. Like I'm the shadow that stretches long across the sidewalk but is never really noticed.

I've found this bench, like an old lover who's stopped asking questions. I sit here every day, watching the city roll by. It's the same parade, day in and day out. The tourists with their camera phones, snapping shots of things they don't understand. The businessmen in their suits, marching toward some destination that doesn't matter. I'm just another part of the background, a blur to them. A piece of the scenery, like the cracked pavement or the piles of trash that gather in the corners. They step around me, but they don't see me. They never see me. And that's fine. I don't need them to.

The city doesn't care, I've learned that now. It doesn't care if I freeze to death or if I die of some disease I can't even pronounce. It won't stop moving for me. It doesn't need me. Hell, it doesn't even notice I'm here. People come and go, but the city keeps breathing. Keeps on growing. Keeps on eating. I'm just another piece of it. Another ghost passing through.

I've stopped asking why. Why I'm still here, why I'm still breathing when everything in me wants to stop. There's no reason. There was never any reason. The people who told me life has meaning, they were full of shit. Life is just a slow crawl to nothingness. The struggle? It's just survival. You fight to stay alive, not because you're fighting for something greater, but because the body refuses to quit. And I guess, in a way, I'm still here because my body's too stubborn to let go.

I think about my death sometimes. It's not some tragic, poetic idea. It's not even something I fear anymore. No, I know better. It'll be quick. A flicker. A shadow in the corner of the street, unnoticed. It won't stop the world. It won't make a difference. And in that, there's a strange kind of peace. I'm not a part of the story. I'm just a footnote. A brief interruption in the city's endless movement. And that's all I'll ever be.

I look at the pigeons picking at the crumbs people leave behind. They've got the same look in their eyes as me. The same hollow, hungry stare. They hop around, scavenging for whatever's left. They've learned that the city doesn't care. It doesn't feed them. They fight for scraps, for survival, and when they're done, they'll die. No one will mourn them. No one will even notice. But they keep going. They keep moving. Because that's what they do. That's what they've learned to do.

I wonder if that's what it is to be human. Not the grand ideas we're told to strive for—success, happiness, fulfillment. No. It's the simple act of moving forward. It's the act of surviving, even when you don't know why. Even when there's no reason. There's no hero's journey for us. There's just this. This endless, grinding, churning motion. And maybe that's the real freedom. The acceptance that we're just bodies, moving through time, scraping against the world until we wear out and fall apart.

I've stopped waiting for a sign. I used to think something would happen, that maybe I'd find a way out, a way to escape. I used to think I'd wake up one day and it'd all make sense. But now? Now, I know better. There's no "better." No grand revelation. There's only the city, and it doesn't give a damn about me. It's too busy devouring everything in its path. It's too busy moving, and I'm just a piece of the wreckage. And that's okay. I've made peace with that.

Sometimes I think I've learned everything I need to know. About the city, about life, about myself. The world doesn't owe me anything. People don't owe me anything. No one's coming to save me, and I'm not asking to be saved. I'm just here. Existing. And maybe that's enough.

I feel it now—the peace that comes with acceptance. The city doesn't care, and neither do I. I don't need to fight anymore. I don't need to demand anything from the world. It is what it is. I am what I am. And in this moment, that's enough. It's the stillness, the absence of need, that makes it all right. Like the weight lifting off my shoulders, just for a second.

The people keep rushing by. The world keeps spinning, as it always has. But I don't feel the pull anymore. I'm not desperate to fit in, not desperate to be noticed. I'm not looking for meaning, because I know now that there is none. There is just this. Just the act of breathing in and out, and maybe, just maybe, that's the most honest thing we can do.

I'll die, eventually. That's certain. But the city will keep moving, like it always does. And when I go, it won't stop. It won't even notice. And that's okay. Because I've accepted that. I've accepted the fact that I'm nothing more than a passing shadow in a place that doesn't care about shadows. And that, strangely, feels like freedom.

I think that's what they mean by peace. To know that nothing matters. To know that life doesn't owe you anything. To know that your death will come, just like everything else. Without fanfare. Without notice. And to be okay with that.

To be okay with the fact that we're all just walking shadows, trying to get by.

Chapter 16: Officer Johnson's Visit

A Cold Confrontation

The bus stop has that strange stillness to it, the kind you only get when the city's half-done with the day but hasn't quite begun the night. The cars hum by, their headlights streaking the sidewalk, flicking shadows across the cracked pavement, like they can't quite be bothered to stop for anything. There's a chill in the air, biting the skin, but I'm too far gone to care about that anymore. It's like the city is too busy moving, too busy shoving me to the edges of its attention, to notice I'm here. To notice me at all.

I've been here before, on this same fucking bench, slouched and forgotten, just another tired soul hoping the night doesn't crush me under its weight. And that's exactly what I am to them—nothing. Just a shadow, a problem to be swept aside when it's no longer convenient.

I light a cigarette, not even bothering to check if I have a lighter. I don't really care. A match strikes from somewhere in my coat pocket. The ember catches, and I take a drag—deep enough to make my lungs burn. I exhale into the streetlights, my breath mixing with the steam from the subway grates, billowing out like smoke signals from a war that no one is fighting anymore.

That's when I see him. Officer Johnson.

At first, I don't even flinch. I've seen him too many times. He's that face—the one that shows up when you're already low, when the city's patience has run out. A patrolman in his mid-forties, with that look in his eyes like he's seen it all, but never enough to make him give a damn. The kind of cop who doesn't ask why you're here, but how quickly he can move you along.

He walks toward me, his boots cracking the pavement like he owns it. His uniform is neat, pressed—an image of order in a world that's anything but. I don't bother with a greeting. There's no point. He never speaks like a human anyway. He speaks like an enforcer. Like the city's rules are gospel and I'm just a sinner.

"You're still here," he says, more like a statement than a question. His voice cuts through the quiet like a blade. It's always the same thing with him—saying nothing, but somehow saying everything.

I lean back against the bench, flicking the ash from my cigarette. My eyes don't meet his, but I can feel the weight of them, like they're waiting for me to say something, anything. As if I'm supposed to explain my existence.

"Yeah," I mutter, not really caring. "Still here."

He lets out a sigh, the kind that sounds like he's exhausted by his own role in this farce. He takes a step closer, his shadow swallowing me whole.

"You're contributing to the problem, you know," he says. There's that same old accusation again. Like I'm some fucking disease that's spreading through his perfect little world. But he doesn't see me. Not really. He sees the thing I represent. The inconvenience. The reality he can't control.

I raise my eyebrows, letting the words hang in the air like smoke.

"Contributing to the problem?" I ask, half laughing. It's bitter, dry. I don't even think he understands how much that statement burns.

He doesn't respond. He just stands there, arms crossed, his jaw clenched in that way that makes you think he's trying not to let his own disgust spill out. He's not angry. No, he's something worse—disillusioned. He's already been here too long. The system's broken, but he's too deep in it to realize it. Or maybe he just doesn't care. Either way, it doesn't matter. I'm just another faceless part of his routine.

"You know," he says, looking around the street like it's some kind of stage, "people are losing their patience with all of you."

"People are losing their patience with the world, Johnson," I reply, my voice low, almost a whisper. "You're just the ones they send out to clean up the mess." I don't look at him. I'm staring at the ground, the concrete, the cracks that go deep into the earth like scars.

He shifts uncomfortably on his feet, the tension hanging between us like a broken wire. It's not what he expected. And it's not what I expected either.

"You think this is your battle?" he snaps, his voice finally breaking with something close to frustration. "You think you're some kind of rebel for doing nothing? You think you're better than the rest of us just 'cause you won't get in line?"

I finally glance up at him, meeting his gaze for the first time. There's nothing there. Just an empty stare, the kind you get from people who've been worn down by the machine. Who've given up on seeing anything real.

"You're just as fucking stuck as I am, Johnson," I say, my voice cold, the words bitter on my tongue. "Only difference is, you've convinced yourself you're the one with the power. But you're just as invisible as me, man. Just wearing a badge instead of rags."

There's a long silence. For a moment, he looks like he's about to speak, but then he doesn't. Instead, he turns and walks away without another word. It's a small victory, I guess. But it's not mine. It's the city's. It's the indifference that does all the work. The city moves on, and so does he, and I'm just left here, still breathing, still waiting.

I take another drag from my cigarette, and the smoke curls around me like the ghosts of everyone who's ever been forgotten by this city. The bus never shows up.

It never does.

The System's Iron Grip

The city's iron grip is a cold thing. It's not something you feel, not the way you feel a lover's hand or the warmth of a coat when the wind cuts through your skin. No, this city's grip is a slow suffocation, something that creeps up on you until your chest feels tight and the breath feels like it's caught in your throat. It's always there, like a shadow you can't escape, even when you close your eyes.

I sit at the bus stop, the glow of my cigarette lighting the night, a last flicker of warmth in a world that's slowly turning cold. The city's quieter now, but it's the kind of quiet that's heavy. It feels like a pause before something terrible happens, like the air's been sucked out and everything's waiting for the hammer to drop. People walk by, their eyes either fixed on the pavement or glued to the screens in their hands. They don't see me. Hell, they couldn't care less.

I've gotten used to it—the invisibility, the cold stares that never come, the way they walk right over you as if you're nothing but a stain on the sidewalk. But still, Officer Johnson always manages to get under my skin. He knows me, but he doesn't see me. He's been around long enough to know that I'm just one more problem for the city to push around. A nuisance. An inconvenience.

The system, that's what they call it—the one that decides who matters and who doesn't, who gets to breathe and who gets to be ground down into dust. It's a machine, a well-oiled beast that grinds you down until you forget your name, your history, your face. You become a thing. A thing to be moved along, to be shoved aside when it's time to clean up. They don't even want to deal with you, but they know they have to. They need you there, just enough for them to point at and say, "This is the problem."

My rights? What the fuck are they in a place like this? In a city that says you're free but locks the doors when you try to get in? The only right I have is the right to survive until they decide I'm no longer useful to them.

I think about it sometimes—what it's like to be a part of the world they're in. To have a place. A purpose. A future. But then I laugh at myself. There's no future for someone like me. No promises, no guarantees. I'm just here, stuck in a limbo where even the concept of "time" is an illusion. The city moves, and I stay put.

Or rather, I get moved. From corner to corner, from one bench to another, just another face in the crowd. But always in the way. Always in someone's way.

Officer Johnson's voice cuts through the thick fog of my thoughts. "You're contributing to the problem." His words come at me like a slap. He's not wrong, but he's not right either. What the hell does he want from me? What does he want from any of us? To disappear? To vanish into the cracks?

And in a way, I've already done that. I've become a ghost—a thing that doesn't really exist, but is just enough of a presence to be ignored, to be dealt with. They don't care what I do, as long as I'm out of their way. But when I'm too visible, too loud, then I'm the problem.

But there's no anger in me anymore. It's not the kind of anger that burns in your chest or makes your fists clench. No, I've traded that for something colder. A kind of exhaustion that sinks deeper into your bones than any rage ever could. What's the point of fighting when the fight is rigged? What's the point of screaming when no one is listening?

People talk about rights. They talk about fairness. They talk about justice. But what's it worth when justice is a product you have to buy? It's a commodity. A luxury. The rich get to wear it like a badge. The poor can only watch as it slips further and further from their reach.

I don't care about justice anymore. I don't care about fairness or rights or anything they tell you you're supposed to care about. They'll lock me up for nothing. They'll throw me in a cage and forget I exist, just like they've forgotten the others. Forgotten all of us who don't fit in their neat little boxes.

But what can I do? There's no answer to that question. I'm not even angry anymore. I've been flattened by the world, worn down until there's nothing left to give. Maybe that's the real crime—the fact that you can be made to disappear so thoroughly that even you forget who you were.

I look down at the cigarette in my hand. It's almost gone. I flick the butt onto the ground, and watch it smolder in the dirt. Will anyone notice when I'm gone? Will they care? Will they even remember me? Or will I just fade out of this city like I never existed?

It doesn't matter. The city doesn't stop moving for anyone. Not for the rich. Not for the poor. Not for the ones who matter or the ones who don't. The only thing the city cares about is its own survival. It'll eat up whatever gets in its way. And if you happen to be one of those things, it'll spit you out like a piece of chewed-up gum.

I finish the last of the cigarette and toss it aside, standing up and brushing the dust off my jeans. I don't have anywhere to go, but I've never really needed a destination. Just a place to be. A place to wait. And wait. And wait.

Because the city doesn't wait for anyone, but it sure does know how to make you wait.

The Shifting Perspective

The words hang in the air long after Officer Johnson's footsteps have faded into the night. "You're contributing to the problem," he said, like he was the first person to ever notice.

I let the sentence bounce around in my head for a while, letting it gnaw at the edges of my thoughts. But the more it stuck to me, the less it meant. There's no indignation left in me. It's like the muscles in my mind have atrophied from too much repetition, too much living without the hope of anything different. If he'd said it three years ago, maybe I would've thrown it back in his face, or at least felt something—anger, defiance, maybe even shame. But now? Now it's just noise. His words a slap that doesn't sting anymore, just a thud against skin that's been hardened to the impact of insults, rejection, and the fact that the only thing that matters here is getting out of the way.

I'm not sure what's worse—the apathy I feel now or the hope I had when I first got here, years ago. I remember walking into the city with the kind of optimism only a desperate man can have, thinking that maybe, just maybe, I could find something real, something that might give me a reason to keep going. But the city doesn't work that way. It doesn't offer salvation. It doesn't care about your dreams or your struggles. All it offers is another broken window to stare out of, another empty bottle to drain, another bench to sleep on while the world moves around you like a silent tide. You're just a part of the scenery, a fixture that can't be removed.

That's what I've become. A fixture. Not a man. Not even a person, really. Just a thing. A thing the system has put in its place.

I keep walking. The streets are quieter now, but they never stop. They're always breathing, always shifting. The endless tide of footsteps, the hum of the city that never turns off, no matter how late it is, no matter how far the lights spill out into the dark. People pass by me like I'm a shadow. I see them, but they don't see me. They walk, they look, but their eyes never meet mine. They look at the ground, their phones, their own thoughts, but they don't see the man sitting at the bus stop, the man who has nowhere else to go. They don't see me.

I've stopped caring whether they do.

You're nothing in this city, unless you're something for someone else. Something to sell, something to consume, something to be used and discarded. I'm neither. I'm just here. A body with no real function, a soul without a purpose.

How many more confrontations will I have with the law before I simply fade into the cracks, another statistic, another nameless casualty of a system that thrives on its own indifference? How long before I become just another forgotten corpse, another number in the obituary column, just a cold face staring back at the world that never noticed me?

Officer Johnson and his like—they're just cogs. Cogs in a machine that's too big for any of us to ever understand. They don't know any better. They don't see the whole picture. They just do their job, and their job is to move people like me out of sight, out of mind, so they can keep walking to their next little piece of the world. They don't care about me. They don't even care enough to hate me. I'm just another part of the problem they've been taught to see, and the solution is simple: get rid of it.

They don't care that I'm human. They don't care that I was someone once, that I had dreams, that I had a family, that I had a life before this. They don't care about any of it.

And why should they? What's my story compared to theirs? I'm just another street rat, a stray dog that doesn't belong in the world they've made. I'm a failure to them. And the thing about failure is that it doesn't just hurt—it makes you disappear. It makes you dissolve into the background. It makes you fade until you're no longer even a person. You're just a thing to be moved, a problem to be dealt with, a nuisance.

I turn down an alley, the smell of piss and garbage cutting through the air. It's quiet back here, away from the main street, away from the eyes of people who never look at you long enough to see anything real. The city hides its filth in places like this, out of sight, but never out of mind. I can feel the coldness seeping into my bones, the kind of cold that comes not from the air but from inside, the kind of cold that never really leaves, that's always there even when you're numb to it.

I think about what I'm supposed to be doing here. What's my purpose in this whole mess? How does a man like me find meaning in a city like this? I'm not fighting for anything anymore. There's no cause to be had, no revolution to fight for, no justice to demand. What's the point of demanding anything from a world that already decided it doesn't care about you? You fight, you scream, you burn out—and they just keep moving, like they always do, and you're left with nothing but ashes in your lungs.

I'm not angry. Not anymore. That kind of fire burns out after a while, and when it's gone, all you're left with is smoke. I've seen too much of it. Seen too many bodies, too many faces like mine, faces that once had dreams, but now are just faces. Worn down to nothing by a system that chews you up and spits you out. I can see the same look in their eyes that I've got in mine. A kind of hollowness, a vacancy, as if the life's been sucked out and replaced with nothing. They've given up fighting. Maybe they never even knew what they were fighting for in the first place.

I'm no different from them. I've given up, too. There's no fight left in me. No passion. No hope.

Just me, walking these streets, another body in the endless line of forgotten souls, just waiting to be buried under the weight of the city's indifference.

It's not even a tragedy anymore. It's just the way things are.

And maybe that's the hardest part to accept. That it doesn't matter if you fight or if you surrender. The city doesn't care. The system doesn't care. They'll grind you down either way. The only thing that's real is that, in the end, you're nothing more than a moment in a machine that's too big for you to ever affect.

So I just keep walking. The lights blur into a haze, the sounds of the city fade to nothing. All that's left is the rhythm of my steps and the weight of the world on my shoulders.

And I don't even bother trying to fight it anymore.

Chapter 17: A Conversation with Marie

Marie's Last Effort

I was sitting in the doorway again. The world around me felt muffled, like the city had wrapped itself in a thick, dirty blanket, and I was the one lying on the cold ground underneath it. The light was fading, but it wasn't like I cared. I didn't care about the cold, or the rats, or the faceless men in suits walking by, pretending I wasn't there. The city always did that—pretended we didn't exist. And I'd learned to pretend right back.

I wasn't even thinking about much, just the hum of the street and the occasional honk of a taxi. My mind was a loop—dark, cyclical, like a song I couldn't turn off. A song that's been stuck in my head for years, and now, I've gotten so used to it, I don't even recognize the words. It just plays on repeat.

Then she appeared.

Marie.

It's been a while.

Days? Weeks? Months? Longer?

I heard her before I saw her—the sound of soft boots on the wet sidewalk. It was like hearing an old friend's voice through a wall. At first, I thought it was just a trick of my brain—something my loneliness conjured up—but no, there she was, standing in front of me, looking at me with those same tired eyes. Same kindness. Same stubborn refusal to walk away.

She was older, yeah. Her face was a little more worn, her hair shorter, and there was a heaviness to her steps now—like life had beaten her too, just like the rest of us. But it wasn't just the years that changed her. It was something else—like she was searching for something in me that I couldn't give her anymore.

"Dez," she said, her voice soft, like she was afraid of breaking something fragile.

I didn't look up. I couldn't.

I could feel her standing there, waiting for me to speak, like I owed her some version of myself that didn't exist anymore. It must have been a long time since I saw her. Too long. She didn't have to come here. She didn't owe me anything. And I didn't owe her a damn thing either.

"Dez," she said again. A little firmer this time. "I got you some coffee."

I looked up then. The cup in her hand looked too clean, too full of warmth. Something I couldn't remember. Something like comfort that I had forgotten how to feel. I didn't take it.

"I'm good," I muttered, staring down at the cracked concrete. "Coffee's not gonna fix anything."

She stood there for a moment, silent. She knew better than to push. She'd learned that over the years. But I could see the faintest flicker of hope in her eyes, something desperate, like she thought I might change for her—just for a second.

"Come on, Dez," she said finally. "Let's just talk. You don't have to do anything. Just talk."

But talking's a lie. What's the point? I'd said it all before, and I wasn't interested in hearing myself speak again. Not to her, not to anyone. Words were just noise bouncing off empty spaces. They didn't fill anything.

I wasn't the man she remembered. I wasn't the one who could laugh at the end of the world or look at her and make her feel like everything was going to be okay. That man had died somewhere in between the cracked sidewalks and the cold nights.

"I don't need to talk," I said, my voice flat. "You can't fix this, Marie. No one can. So don't waste your time."

She didn't argue with me. She never did. Not anymore. She'd tried to reach me once, maybe twice before, but this time, it felt different. There was a tiredness in her eyes—like she knew the fight was over. Like she was standing there not out of hope, but because she had to. Maybe this was her last try. Maybe she wasn't just trying to save me. She was trying to save herself from the guilt of giving up.

"You don't have to go back out there," she said. "There's a shelter near here. Just a few blocks away. You don't have to stay out here in the cold. Just a few hours, Dez. Please."

I could feel the sincerity in her voice, and I wanted to scream at her. Scream that it didn't matter. That it would never matter. I wanted to tell her that there was no "out there" for people like me. That the shelter she was offering me would just be another cage, another place to sit and wait for the inevitable. A place to disappear slowly while they filed away my name in some database.

But I didn't.

Instead, I just shook my head, the movement so small, it barely made a ripple in the air.

"No. I'm fine here."

I could see her struggling with something, a thought, a piece of herself that wanted to beg, but she wouldn't. She couldn't. She wasn't stupid. She knew the world didn't work that way. She knew no matter how much you begged, you couldn't change the way things were. The way people like me were made to disappear.

"I wish I could help you, Dez," she whispered, as if saying it aloud might make the words come true.

Her voice cracked like a broken record, and for a second, I almost let myself feel something. Almost.

"You can't," I said quietly, my voice rougher now. "I can't even help myself anymore."

She stood there for a long time, just looking at me. There was nothing left to say. She'd tried, and I'd rejected her. I'd rejected everything.

"I'll leave the coffee here, then," she said, setting the cup down next to me.

I didn't move.

She lingered for a moment longer, but I didn't look up again.

When she left, I sat there, the cup of coffee growing colder next to me. It didn't matter. Nothing mattered. Not anymore. Not the shelter, not the coffee, not the kindness she still had for me.

I could almost hear the sound of her footsteps fading away. It felt final. Like the end of a story no one would remember.

I didn't pick up the coffee. I didn't even look at it.

And when I finally closed my eyes, the cold felt a little heavier than before.

The Wall Between Them

I'm sitting on the stoop of some building. The kind of building that's seen better days, long ago, when there was a time it meant something. Or maybe it never did. Hell, buildings don't care. It's just stone and brick and glass—lifeless, like the people that surround them. I could care less about the damn building, or the street, or the city, but they're here and they're mine. At least for now.

I feel the weight of the air like I always do: thick with indifference. It presses down on my chest like a hundred invisible hands. The world doesn't even try to hide it anymore. It's like they've all just agreed: "You're not really here, Dez. You're just something in the way. Something to get around."

Marie's voice cuts through the hum of traffic. She's standing there, looking at me like she's trying to break through the concrete wall I've built around myself. It's a tired look—she's worn down by me, I can see that. Her eyes, the same eyes that used to hold so much hope for me, now just want to hold on to something.

Something that I can't give her. She's got a coffee in her hand, steam rising from it, the kind of thing people do when they think they can save someone.

She offers me the cup. "Dez, it's freezing out here. You should come inside for a while."

I shake my head. It's not the cold that's eating at me. It's the emptiness. It's the knowledge that I'm beyond saving. Her words are like snowflakes—they melt on contact with the ground and disappear, leaving nothing behind.

"I'm fine," I mutter. It's a lie. I'm not fine. I'm beyond fine. I'm nothing.

She takes a step closer, but there's no warmth in her eyes anymore. Not really. She's been through this before—knows how it goes. I'll reject her, I'll push her away, and she'll try again, and we'll do this dance until we're both too tired to move.

"You don't have to do this alone, Dez," she says. Her voice cracks. I almost feel bad. Almost.

"I've been doing it alone for years, Marie," I snap, looking up at her. "What makes you think it's gonna change now? It's all the same. Same streets. Same dirt. Same face in the mirror every morning. It doesn't get better. It doesn't get easier."

She hesitates, like the words are too heavy for her. She lowers the coffee, staring down at it like she's trying to figure out what went wrong. She's been trying to fix me for too long. There's no fixing me. There's nothing left to fix.

"I'm just trying to help," she says, but the words feel empty. They've lost their meaning.

I laugh. It's bitter, dry. "Help? You think a shelter or some food is gonna change anything? It's not. It never was. This life isn't something you get saved from, Marie. It's something you survive. And you do it alone, or you don't do it at all."

Her shoulders slump, and I feel the tension between us snap like a taut rope. She's finally starting to understand. Maybe she always knew. Maybe that's why she never stayed. The idea of me broke her, little by little, and now she's just trying to make sure there's something left of her before she walks away.

But she can't save me, and she knows it. She knows I've already disappeared.

"You're still here," she says quietly, more to herself than to me.

The words hang in the air, and for a second, I almost believe them. But then they vanish, like everything else. Because there's nothing left to believe in.

I push myself off the stoop, the cold biting into my skin. "You should go, Marie," I say, my voice quieter now. "You've got your life. Don't waste it on me."

Her lips tremble, like she's holding back some dam of tears that won't stop once they break free. But she doesn't cry. She doesn't say anything else. She just turns and walks away.

Her steps are slow, like she's trying to drag the moment out, trying to hold on to something that isn't there. I watch her until she fades into the crowd, just another face in the sea of people who don't see me.

And then I'm alone again. Alone in a city that doesn't give a damn. Alone in a world that doesn't care.

But I've always been alone, haven't I?

There's no room for hope anymore. No room for fixing what's already broken. This is the only truth I know now: you survive, or you die. There's no middle ground.

And I'm still here, so I guess I'm surviving.

But I can feel it slipping away. That last piece of me that used to want something more. It's gone.

And it's never coming back.

Dez's Moment of Truth

I sit there, my back pressed against the cold concrete like some forgotten relic of the city. The coffee's gone lukewarm, but I'm still holding the cup, like it might magically give me a jolt of life or something. It doesn't. It's just a cup. The warmth it gave me when Marie handed it over is already gone, evaporated with the steam. And what's left? Nothing but my hands trembling around a cheap paper cup, the skin of my palms puckered from the weight of years spent clawing at nothing.

I can feel the city moving around me—horns honking, the screech of tires, the rhythm of footsteps, the muffled hum of someone's headphones as they zip by. It's all there, just outside my reach. Life. It's happening to everyone else but me.

I've spent too many years pushing people away. Not just Marie. Everyone. Everyone who's ever tried to help me. They all get the same treatment. I don't need their pity. I don't need their sympathy. I don't need anyone.

I'm sick of their goddamn help. Sick of their empty offers, their promises that they'll "help me get clean," like they have any fucking clue what that even means. Help me get clean? Clean from what? The dirt on my skin? The dirt in my veins? Or the dirt in my soul?

I've built walls around me, and every brick is one more denial, one more "fuck you" to the world. And Marie? She doesn't get it. She thinks she's gonna save me with a cup of coffee and a couple of words. But all she's really done is prove me right. She gave up. Not on me, maybe, but on the idea of me ever changing. She's as lost as I am, just hiding behind a different set of lies.

I stare at the street—cars, people, the parade of faces that never notice me. None of them see the shit I've had to deal with. None of them know how it feels to be invisible, to live in the cracks of the pavement like some rat scurrying through the city's arteries.

Marie leaves. She says something about hoping I'll think about what she said, but I'm already tuning her out. She's already gone. I watch her walk down the block, her back a little straighter than it was when she approached me, and I can almost hear her thinking, I tried. He didn't want it. I can't help him anymore. And it's true. She can't. Nobody can.

Hell, I've known that for years. I've known it deep down, in the marrow of my bones. I'm past the point of no return. I'm waiting for the end, the slow suffocating crawl toward oblivion. Maybe that's what life is: just waiting for death, while pretending the waiting is something worth doing.

But what's the point? I can't find meaning in anything anymore. I can't find meaning in anything but the slow drip of the day. The constant shuffle of feet on the sidewalk. The scrape of trash against the curb. The guttering of a neon sign across the street. It's all the same.

Marie wanted to save me. But she doesn't understand. She doesn't know that saving me would mean prolonging my suffering. She's not saving me, she's just stretching out the agony. There's no escape from this. No white knight coming to pull me out of the gutter. Just the gutter. And it's fine.

The city hums on around me. Life moves. But I'm nothing but a stain on the side of it, a side-effect of whatever fucked-up thing this city is supposed to be. I watch the people around me go about their business, pretending to be alive, pretending like they're really doing something. But I know they're just as empty as I am. They're just better at hiding it. They wear their masks, the ones with the smiles and the nice clothes. They're no better than me.

Maybe that's the worst part. The lie that we're all living some grand story, when really we're just passing the time until the inevitable. Life is just a series of distractions to keep us from staring into the void too long.

I watch the city buzz with life and death, and for the first time, I realize—there's no difference. Life is a city. Death is a city. Everything moves, but nothing changes.

I think about Marie. I think about her face, the way she looked at me like I might still matter. But I don't. Not to her. Not to anyone. She doesn't know this version of me. She remembers the one I used to be—the guy with the spark in his eyes, the guy who could still smile at the right moment, the guy who could pretend that something good was coming. But that guy's gone. He died a long time ago, buried under the weight of a thousand bad decisions.

The coffee cup is empty now, and I toss it aside like I've tossed everything else away. The city roars on, the same as it ever was. No different from yesterday. No different from tomorrow.

I'm alone in the middle of it, and that's all there is. That's all there will ever be.

I'll die here. Probably soon. Maybe in my sleep. Maybe in the gutter, face down in the wet concrete.

It doesn't matter. I don't care.

But that's the lie, isn't it?

I care. I care too much.

Chapter 18: Dez's Choice

The Crossroads

The rain falls hard. Cold sheets that slap against my skin and make the concrete slick beneath my feet. The city's soaked, dripping, and the people—goddamn people—they keep moving, heads down, umbrellas up, rushing past me like I'm not even here.

I don't know why I'm standing here. What the hell am I waiting for? Some kind of miracle? Some flash of meaning? It's all just smoke, all of it. I see the faces—no one's looking at me, and I don't want them to. But I can't help but notice how they don't even see me. Like I'm a shadow, a shape that doesn't belong.

I'm not even sure what I'm doing here anymore.

The traffic lights flicker—red to green to yellow. They don't mean anything. They don't signal a goddamn thing. I'm not going anywhere. And I'm not sure I even want to. I've been walking these streets for how long now? Five years, ten? Doesn't matter. There's nothing new left to see. The pavement's as familiar as my own skin, but I'm just as lost as I was the first time I got here.

And this damn rain. It's the only thing that touches me. The cars zoom by like they've got somewhere important to be. The people, they scurry past like they're racing against something—time, death, a chance at redemption. They don't even know what they're running from. They wouldn't know the first thing about it.

I can't feel the rain anymore. My skin's numb. My bones ache from too many cold nights spent wrapped in layers of grime and broken promises.

What the hell does it mean to survive, anyway? What am I still hanging on to? This fight isn't even a fight anymore. I'm just here, breathing in air that's not mine to breathe. I used to tell myself that if I just made it through one more day, one more week, that maybe—maybe—I'd figure out some way to make sense of this shit. But that's a lie. A big one. I've spent too many years chasing a goddamn nothing, and now I'm just too tired to keep running.

I'm not sure if I'm waiting for someone to come and save me anymore. That's what Marie thought she was doing. She came here with that bullshit hope in her eyes, thinking that if she just threw me a little help, a little care, I'd turn into something better. She didn't get it. She didn't get me.

No one does.

I used to think that people could change you, or at least pull you out of the muck long enough to see the sky. But it's all just a joke. I tried. I really did. But now, I see the truth. People are just like cars, they drive past you, and the minute you're not in front of them, they forget you. They forget you like you were never there at all.

I don't want to change. And that's the hardest part of it. I've made my peace with the fact that I'm a lost cause. There's no going back now.

The rain keeps coming, falling harder, louder. The city hums with life, with movement, with noise. But none of it means anything. People walk past me like I'm a ghost. And I wonder, in the back of my mind, what it would feel like to just disappear.

No one would even care.

Maybe I'll cross the street. Maybe I won't. What does it matter? The choice seems meaningless now. Cross, don't cross, live, die, breathe, stop. It's all the same. I'm already dead inside. I've been dead for years.

But I'm still here, standing in the rain, feeling every drop like it's the only thing left keeping me tied to this miserable existence. There's something in the repetition of it that feels like a punishment, but I can't tell if I deserve it anymore.

You know what they say—every choice matters. But they're wrong. Some choices don't matter. They're just the illusion of choice, a way to keep you moving when you've already stopped. Maybe I'm still here because I'm waiting for something to give me a reason to keep going. Or maybe I'm just too fucking tired to end it all. Either way, I don't have the energy to care.

I used to be angry at the world. Angry at Marie for not saving me, angry at the city for eating me alive. But now I'm just tired. Tired of the noise, tired of the people, tired of this goddamn city that chews you up and spits you out and then forgets your name the minute you're out of sight.

And I'm standing here, drenched, watching it all. Waiting for something that's never going to come.

A Final Decision

I'm walking now, letting the rain slap at my face, the wet air sticking to the back of my neck like a bad memory. I don't have a destination. I don't need one. I'm not moving toward anything. I'm just moving because that's what you're supposed to do, right? Keep moving, keep existing, keep pretending like there's something worth moving toward. But I don't believe in that anymore.

I walk past the usual shit—the storefronts, the cabs honking at pedestrians who don't care, the drunks arguing with the air. There's nothing new here. Nothing I haven't seen a thousand times before. I used to think the city had a heartbeat, that there was something alive in the way it moved, but now all I see are hollowed-out shells, filled with people who don't look at each other, don't look at me, and sure as hell don't look at themselves.

I don't know why I'm still here. What's the point? A man can only bleed so much, right? You ever think about how, when you're on the streets, time doesn't really exist? There's no days, no hours. It's just a blur of cold, of hunger, of wasted time spent in spaces too small for your soul. And you begin to wonder—does it even matter? Does it matter if I make it through the night, or if I don't? What's left to fight for?

I remember Ana. I remember Stevie. God, I miss her, I miss them. But the thing is, they're gone now. Long gone. And I wonder, in some corner of my broken heart, if it wouldn't be easier if they never existed at all. If I hadn't known love, or friendship, or connection. If I hadn't seen a glimmer of warmth in the dark, I wouldn't have to sit here in the cold, watching the world keep spinning without me.

That's what happens when you let people in. You get attached. And then you get burned. I let Ana into my life, and she walked away like I was nothing. Same with Stevie. Everyone does. You spend all this time pretending you matter, and then one day you're just a face in the crowd. You think people are going to save you, but the truth is, no one's coming for you. Not now, not ever.

Maybe death would be a release. A kind of permanent vacation from this shit-show called life. I could lay down and just sleep forever. No more struggle. No more pain. No more cold. No more hunger gnawing at my stomach like a rat.

I reach a park bench, the one I always sit at when I need to think. I don't know why I come here. Maybe it's because, even though the city never stops, this park always feels like it's in a permanent state of pause. The grass is wet, the trees are bent by the wind, but it all feels still, like time stopped ticking here. And maybe that's what I want. A moment where nothing matters.

I sit down, my coat wet, my pants soaked through, but I don't care. I feel the weight of everything pressing against me. Every loss, every regret, every dream I buried alive. The emptiness is a wall now, thick and unbreakable. People walk by, wrapped up in their own little worlds, and I wonder—do they even know how much they're missing?

The city, the streets, the buildings—they're all just a backdrop for the real thing, the thing that matters. The loneliness. That's what's real.

I think about Marie. She tried, didn't she? She gave me that coffee, she sat with me, talked to me like I was a person. But what did it matter? She doesn't know. She doesn't get it. People don't get it.

And then I think—maybe she did get it. Maybe she saw through me. Maybe she saw the walls I've built around myself, and she knew I'd never break down. It's easier to walk away than to try and fix something that's already beyond saving.

I watch a pigeon pecking at crumbs on the ground, its feathers ruffled, its eyes vacant. I see myself in that bird. Pecking at scraps, moving on instinct, because there's nothing else to do. It doesn't matter that the crumbs are stale. It doesn't matter that there's no real food, no real sustenance. We keep going because we have to. That's the only thing we know how to do—keep going.

But what if stopping is better? What if laying down and letting the world keep spinning without me is a kind of freedom? Maybe that's what I've been waiting for all this time. For the permission to just stop.

I light a cigarette. The flicker of the flame is brief, swallowed by the wetness of the air. The smoke curls around me, thick, heavy, and it feels like everything is closing in on me. But it's comforting, in a way. It's the only thing I've got left. Smoke and ash. The brief illusion of warmth.

I think of the people who've passed through my life—friends, lovers, strangers. They're gone now, just like everyone else. Some people think they can save you, but they're wrong. You can't save a person who doesn't want to be saved. I stopped wanting to be saved a long time ago.

It's not that I'm giving up. I'm just tired.

The noise of the city, the sound of tires on wet pavement, it all blends together, a dull hum in the background of my thoughts. I wonder if it'll ever stop. I wonder if I'll ever get to a place where I'm not always thinking about survival. About hunger. About cold. About pain. Maybe that's the problem. Maybe I've never really lived. Maybe I've just been surviving.

So what happens if I stop surviving?

What happens if I decide to let go?

I close my eyes for a moment. The rain still falls, soft but steady. It's the only thing that feels real, the only thing that keeps me tethered to this moment. And in the silence, I know.

The choice is mine.

Survival has no meaning anymore. It's just a game we play, a lie we tell ourselves to keep going when we don't have anything left to give. But I'm tired of playing. I'm tired of the lie. And maybe it's time to stop pretending.

So I sit there, in the rain, and I wait. Not for the world to change, not for something to happen, but for the moment when I can finally make my decision.

Acceptance of Death

The city's noises are louder now, a mess of honks, footsteps, and the metallic screech of buses pulling to a halt. The sun's gone down, and the streetlights flicker on like faulty candles in a drafty room. They throw long shadows across the pavement, shadows that remind me of things I can't quite touch anymore. Time's running out, but it doesn't matter. It's the way it was always going to end.

I've been sitting here for God knows how long. Maybe an hour, maybe more. Doesn't matter. The chill in the air is starting to settle into my bones. I don't feel the hunger gnawing at my stomach, or the ache in my joints from sleeping on benches for days on end. I don't feel much of anything anymore. I'm just here. Just existing. And that's the only thing I know now.

I look up, and the faces pass me by—some lost in their phones, some lost in their thoughts, others just blank. I know them, even if they don't know me. They all keep moving, all trying to make their way somewhere. Somewhere that doesn't matter. I used to think they were the ones with it all figured out, but now I see them for what they are: just people running toward their own oblivion. Just like me.

I take a drag from the cigarette, watch the smoke swirl in the air and disappear. I'm trying to figure out when it happened—the moment I stopped caring about anything. I think it was gradual, like the slow buildup of dust on a shelf that you don't notice until it's choking you. Maybe it started when Ana left. Maybe it was when Stevie died. Maybe it was before that, when the weight of it all started to crush me and I realized I wasn't built for this world, never was.

I used to think death was a way out. Something to fear, something to run from, like some predator lurking in the alley behind me. But tonight, sitting here on this damn bench, I don't fear it. Not anymore. I've seen it too many times, had it stare me down in the faces of the junkies and the drunks who don't make it through the night. I've seen it in the hollow eyes of the old man pushing his shopping cart full of cans. And I've seen it in my own reflection every time I pass a storefront window.

Death isn't the enemy anymore. It's just a part of it all. The final punctuation on a sentence that doesn't matter. I think the hardest part wasn't dying—it was surviving. It's surviving when there's nothing left, when your body's just a machine running on fumes, and you've got no fuel to keep going. But you do it anyway, like a goddamn zombie, because that's the game. You play, you play, you play until you can't play anymore.

But tonight, I'm done with the game.

I close my eyes for a second, feeling the cool breeze cut through me like a blade. There's a moment there, just for a second, where the noise of the city falls away and all I hear is my heartbeat. That dull thud that's been with me all my life. It's slowing down now, like it knows something I don't. Or maybe it knows exactly what I do. That it's over. That it was always over.

I don't know what's next. No one does. People talk about it like they've got some great answer—like they know what happens when you breathe your last breath. Heaven, hell, reincarnation. But all I know is that for the first time in a long time, I'm okay with the not-knowing.

It's not about escape anymore. There's no romanticism in it, no dramatic moment. Death is just the end of this cycle. The moment when the world stops spinning around you. When you stop pretending there's a reason to keep fighting, when you stop fooling yourself into thinking that one more day of struggle will make it all worth it.

The wind picks up, rustling the leaves from the trees above me. I feel a shiver run through me, but it's not the cold. It's something else. A kind of release. Maybe it's the release I've been waiting for. Maybe I've been holding my breath for so long, thinking it was all going to get better, that I forgot how to breathe without the weight of it all on me. I take in a deep breath now. And for the first time in years, it doesn't hurt.

There's a quiet here that's different from the usual noise of the city. A quiet that feels heavy. Like the kind of quiet you get when someone's about to tell you something important but never does. Like the weight of everything you could've said but never said. But for once, I'm okay with the silence. The city hums around me, but the hum feels like a lullaby, like a soft whisper telling me it's time to let go.

I've been waiting for this moment. The moment when I wouldn't have to fight anymore. The moment when I wouldn't have to pretend. Pretend that the pain was worth it, that the cold was worth it, that any of it was worth it. And now, sitting on this damn bench in the middle of a city that's forgotten me, I realize that it never was.

The world keeps moving. The people keep walking. The city keeps breathing, a never-ending pulse that can't hear me, can't see me. But I don't care.

Because death doesn't give a shit about your plans. It doesn't ask for your permission. It just comes, like a storm that sweeps you up in its winds, whether you're ready or not. And right now, I'm not fighting it. I'm not running from it. I'm just waiting for it to come, and when it does, I'll welcome it like an old friend, a friend who's always known where I've been.

I look around one last time. The light flickers above me, casting long shadows across the pavement. The air smells like wet concrete, like trash, like the remnants of all the people who came before me and left their mark.

And then I close my eyes again, the cool breeze brushing against my skin, and for the first time in a long time, I feel at peace.

Chapter 19: The End of the Road

A Quiet Departure

I don't know what happened. One minute, I was walking, breathing, barely existing, and the next—nothing. I mean, nothing at all. I didn't even get the chance to feel it coming. No grand "final act," no fanfare. Just a slow fade. Death isn't some dramatic finish like in the movies, where people rush to your side with tears in their eyes, begging you not to go. It's just... quiet. You slip away like a worn-out sock dropped in a dark corner of the room. Unnoticed. No one cares.

I'm sitting on this bench—god knows where exactly, somewhere near the bottom of the world, somewhere that doesn't matter anymore. Maybe an alley, maybe a park. Hell, it could be a subway platform. The truth is, I don't know. My back hurts, my legs are numb, and the cold is creeping in deeper, slicing through my skin. I'm stiff with it, like a carcass caught in the first frost. But I don't mind anymore. What's it matter? Life was always a grind, always a game of pretending you could make it out, pretending you could keep moving. But the truth is—no one's getting out. The city will eat you alive, spit you out, and keep on moving like you were never here.

I've been here so long I've become part of the furniture. A fixture. Just another blur in the crowd, blending into the urban sprawl, another nameless face among thousands. I never wanted to be anyone's hero. I never wanted to be a symbol of anything, not even a tragedy. I just wanted a way out. I thought maybe, just maybe, someone would pull me up from this muck. But no. Ana's gone. Stevie too. And me? I'm still here, but only because I haven't had the decency to drop dead yet.

The city's humming, just like it always does. Cars screaming by, tires screeching, people arguing, laughing, talking. There's a whole orchestra going on out there—honks, shouts, the rattling of subway trains, the sounds of a thousand tiny lives intersecting and overlapping in a place that couldn't give less of a shit if any of us lived or died. The cacophony of it all used to drive me crazy, but now? Now it's just background noise. Like static on an old radio. You stop hearing it after a while. It becomes part of the air, part of the dirt you breathe in and out. But the thing is—the air's getting heavier. My chest feels tight, and I'm not sure if it's the cold, the exhaustion, or the thought that the end is coming. I'm not even scared anymore. I'm just tired.

I can feel the weight of it now—the weight of all the things I never said, never did. All the chances I let slip by. All the nights spent in places like this, thinking that maybe tomorrow, maybe just tomorrow, things would be different. But that's bullshit. Tomorrow's just another lie we tell ourselves to keep the wheels turning. It doesn't come, and when it does, it's just another version of the same tired shit.

Ana, she used to tell me I was too far gone. She said I wasn't built for this life. Maybe she was right. Maybe I was never meant to be part of the living, part of the world where people walk around pretending they've got something worth holding on to. But she's gone now, and it doesn't matter. It never really did. She thought I could save her, that we could both get out, together. But there's no getting out, not really. Not if you've lived here long enough to know the truth.

The wind picks up, and I feel it biting my skin like a thousand needles. It cuts through my worn jacket, through the hole in my shoes, into the marrow of my bones. I can smell it now—the air in the city, thick with exhaust, the tang of rotten food, the sharp metallic scent of broken dreams. It makes me want to throw up. But it doesn't matter. I could puke right here on this bench, and no one would care. They'd just walk by, like they always do, pretending not to see.

It's funny how people can be so damn close to each other, and yet, they're so far away. I've sat on these benches, watched people pass me by, and not once did I feel connected. They all look right through me, like I'm a ghost, like I don't even exist. And you know what? Maybe I don't. Maybe that's the point. Maybe I'm not meant to be here.

I think about Stevie for a second. He was always laughing, always cracking jokes like he didn't care about anything, like he had it all figured out. He was a good man, but you know what? I'm not sure he understood the way this place really worked. He didn't get that it's not about fighting or winning. It's about surviving. It's about trying to get through one more day without losing your mind, without letting the city swallow you whole. And now he's gone—forever out of reach. And more and more the weight of his name fades like smoke into a sky that doesn't care.

I used to care about things—about survival, about finding food, about staying warm—but that was years ago. Now? It's just the same day, stretched out over and over again. Same bench. Same people walking by, not seeing me, not caring. Same garbage trucks rumbling through the streets. Same endless noise, just louder. I used to wish for something different. A different life. A different world. But now? I don't wish for anything. Not anymore. The cold's too deep, the darkness too thick.

I let my eyes close, just for a second, just to escape it all. And for a moment, there's nothing. No honking, no fighting, no sirens. Just silence. It feels good. Not the kind of good that fills you up, but the kind of good that comes when you stop fighting. When you stop pretending that you're going to make it out of here alive.

And then, for the first time in what feels like forever, I feel at ease. Not peaceful, but at ease. The way you feel when you stop thinking, when you stop wondering if there's more. I've been fighting my whole life to survive, but the fight's over now.

I open my eyes, and the city's still there. Same ugly, sprawling mess. Same indifferent, soulless thing that it's always been. But I don't care anymore. The sky's darker now, that purple-gray color of dusk, and I don't even look up. It doesn't matter. I've lost interest in the sky, in the clouds, in the horizon. I'm just here, sitting on this bench, letting the city pass me by, one day at a time.

And if no one notices me go? If no one even cares that I'm gone?

Well, that's just how it goes.

The City's Unyielding Momentum

I'm gone now, just like I knew I would be. Disappeared, like all the others who sit too long in the shadows, asking for spare change or a moment of dignity. But nobody notices when you're gone, not really. The city doesn't care, and that's the truth of it. It just keeps turning, grinding everything down to dust and making sure that whatever you were doesn't matter anymore.

The body's cold now, rotting quietly somewhere—maybe in a back alley, maybe stuffed under a blanket in the park, or maybe they just kicked me to the curb, like they always do. Who knows? Who cares? I don't even care. Because it's over. The life I lived—the one where I begged for food and warmth and hope—has burned out. And it wasn't even with a bang, no dramatic exit. No one will miss me. No one will even blink.

I'm just another piece of trash, waiting to be swept up.

The city's an unforgiving machine, like some kind of ugly monster with its teeth grinding away. It chews and chews, spits out the broken ones, and swallows them whole. And when those broken ones die, there's no grand moment of silence, no memorials, no standing ovation for the soul that gave up. No, the world keeps marching on. The trains keep rattling. The lights keep flashing. And the street cleaners do their jobs.

They found my body eventually—probably just some worker walking the beat, bored, looking for something to do. They didn't see me as a person; I wasn't a tragedy. I was just another lost one—a name on a sheet of paper they forgot the moment they marked it down. It's easy to do that when you don't care, when you can't even remember the people who cross your path on the way to the next thing.

The thing about this city, and I've seen it for years now, is that it's a *machine*. And people? They're parts. You're not a person here. You're a cog. And when you break down, they just replace you. A new one. Fresh, shiny, ready for the grind.

You see it every day. The rich ones who walk past you, never looking. They've got their heads buried in their phones or their coffee cups. They don't even see you. And why would they? You're not part of their world. You're not a part of their reality. You're a background noise. A thing that doesn't matter, a blemish on their clean little world.

And that's what it's all about. You're just a forgotten echo, a piece of furniture, a spare part to be ignored and replaced. I used to think that if I could just make a mark somehow—just scream, or fight, or hurt somebody—maybe they'd remember. But that's not how it works. They don't care. Not really. And in the end, they don't even notice when you're gone. It's like you never existed.

I'm no different than the others, no different than all the other nameless souls who died in the streets. I was born here, raised here in the gutter, and in the gutter, I died. That's how it goes. I can't even say I was special. I can't even say I had something that deserved a mention, because I didn't.

The world just keeps moving. People walk on by, heads down, eyes fixed ahead. Their feet tap out rhythms they don't even know. They're so damn busy running to the next thing that they don't even have time to think about you. And why should they? They've got their jobs, their families, their debts. Their *busy* little lives. You're not part of it. You're just the guy who sits on the corner with a sign. And when you die? You're gone. That's all.

And there's something beautiful in that, if you're ready for it. The complete indifference. The nothingness. It's like a weight off your shoulders, knowing that in the end, you don't matter. You don't have to try anymore. You don't have to make a difference or leave a legacy. It's all going to disappear. Just like me. Just like the others. Like the trash that gets picked up at the end of the day.

People live their lives like they're going to leave some kind of mark on this world, like the world's going to stop and say, "Look at what you did." But that's not how it goes. The world doesn't care about you. It doesn't care about your dreams, your fears, or your stupid little struggles. It doesn't care if we fall. The only thing it cares about is keeping the machine going. The people in their shiny shoes and pressed suits, they just walk by, pretending that they're better than the rest of us. They act like they don't know that they're just one bad break away from being in the same spot. But they don't stop. They don't think about it.

I was never anything more than a blip, a shadow, a flicker in the dark. But now I'm gone. Just another face nobody remembers. Maybe someone will walk past this spot and wonder where I went. Maybe they'll even stop for a second and wonder about the guy on the bench. But they won't. They don't have time. They've got their own lives to live, their own problems to solve. And in the end, it doesn't matter. Because it was never about me.

It was never about any of us.

The city will sweep the streets, it'll keep turning. And somewhere in the distance, someone will replace me. And when I'm forgotten, like every other forgotten soul in this city, it won't be a tragedy. It'll just be the *next thing*. And then, it'll be their turn. To disappear.

Stuck

I don't know if it was the whiskey or the crack or just life grinding its teeth, but there's a part of me that's still stuck on it. Maybe it was something I could've done. Maybe I could've changed something. I remember the nights I sat in the alley behind that bar on 56th Street. Cold wind cutting through the rags on my back, looking up at the neon signs flickering above me. "Hope," one said, some tacky thing about salvation. And I remember thinking, "If hope's a sign, then maybe I'm just standing in the wrong alley."

But it didn't matter, did it? Hope doesn't last. It's just another drug, another reason to keep dragging your ass out of bed every morning. But all you're really doing is circling the drain, faster and faster, until one day it all ends.

So I drank, I smoked, I let the machine swallow me whole. I tried to make sense of it, but I couldn't. And now? Well, I don't know. Maybe I was too tired to fight it anymore. Maybe I just couldn't keep running in place.

I tried to remember what it felt like when I had hope, but that was a long time ago, back when I was a kid. Maybe that's why I still feel something in the pit of my stomach when I think of those nights in the alley. It was the last shred of something real, something raw. A memory of me, not this broken-down version that's left behind. But it doesn't change anything. The city keeps moving, the rich get richer, the poor get poorer, and I fade into the background like a shadow nobody cares about.

A Moment of Reflection

The last few days are a blur now—like a bad dream I can't wake up from. The city hums around me, always moving, always pushing. I'm just one more forgotten piece of garbage in its machine, but that's how it's always been, right?

I was never meant to last, just a flash in the night, a ripple in the ocean, nothing more than a smudge on the concrete. I can't say I'm sorry. Not for myself anyway. I've lived this way so long, breathing in the piss-scented air, watching the same faces shuffle past, blank and indifferent. It's a weird kind of freedom, really. They don't expect anything from you. They don't ask you to be anyone but what you are—nobody. There's a twisted kind of peace in that. The thing is, they don't care when you're gone, either. They just sweep you away, make the streets shiny again, put a fresh coat of paint on everything. Like I never even existed.

I used to think it would matter. I used to think someone—maybe Ana—would remember me. But no one does. I've seen the same thing happen a thousand times. A body's found in an alley, wrapped in its own despair, and the next day, the same shitty people are walking by like nothing happened. No one remembers the ghosts. We're all just part of the scenery, the backdrop of their lives, but nobody stops to notice. We're like cracked pavement, graffiti, broken lights—part of the city's soul, but invisible.

Sometimes I wonder if anyone would've cared if I'd done things differently. Maybe if I had a job, a suit, a house with a white picket fence. Maybe if I hadn't trusted the wrong people, or hadn't let the years chew me up. But then I laugh at myself, a dry, bitter laugh, because that's the joke, isn't it? The whole damn thing's rigged. The cards were stacked against me from the start, but I was too dumb to see it. The dream they sell you, the one about hard work and perseverance—it's a lie. Only the ones already inside the house get the benefit of that lie. The rest of us? We just scrape by, waiting for the inevitable. And when we die, we die alone, like forgotten animals in the street.

No, it wouldn't have mattered. Not for me. Not for anyone like me.

I think of Ana sometimes. I wonder if she ever thinks of me. Probably not. She's built herself a life, maybe kids by now, a whole world of her own that doesn't include me. People like me don't fit into those worlds. We're stains on their carpet, easily ignored, scrubbed out when it's convenient. I can't say I blame her. I wouldn't want to be dragged down by someone like me, either.

But still, there's that part of me, the one that's been dying for years, that holds onto the hope that maybe—just maybe—I'll find a reason to matter. That I'll mean something to someone, somewhere. But that's the thing, isn't it? We're all hoping for meaning in a world that doesn't care. We build these little worlds inside our heads, and fill them with stories about ourselves, but none of it matters. Not in the end. Not really. Not when the streets are full of us, discarded, forgotten.

It's strange, isn't it? You live your whole life searching for something—some spark, some connection, some reason to believe you're not just a waste of space—and then one day it stops. You stop. Like a broken clock, still ticking but no longer keeping time. And then—nothing. Just silence.

I don't know how long I've been sitting here, in this alley, watching the world move past me like I'm invisible. I'm used to it now, the loneliness. It's the kind of pain that sneaks up on you. At first, it's the kind of sting—sharp, immediate, unbearable—but then it settles in. Like a dull ache that never quite goes away.

The kind of pain you get used to. The kind that becomes part of you. I've been carrying it so long, I don't even know what it feels like to not be alone anymore.

I can't tell you when I stopped fighting, when I stopped caring. Maybe it was after the first winter in the shelter, crammed in with a hundred other guys, all of us wrapped in our misery, our hunger, our sickness. Or maybe it was when I realized that no matter what I did, the world would never care. It doesn't care about the people who fall through the cracks. It doesn't care about the ones who live in the shadows, the ones who don't fit into its pretty picture.

So I learned to disappear. I learned to blend into the backdrop, to become just another part of the city's machinery. It's easier that way. And it's easier still when you know you don't matter.

But here's the thing—I don't even know if I'm afraid to die anymore. I think I've been dying for a long time. Every day I wake up, and the world hasn't changed. Every day I feel my body getting older, weaker, more worn down. It's like I'm already gone. Maybe death's just the final exhale. The last moment of release, when you finally let go of everything that weighs you down. Maybe it's not so bad. Maybe it's the only escape.

But there's no grand ending to my story. No tragic finale. No moment where everything suddenly makes sense. Just the sound of the city. The endless drone of cars, people, noise. And then the fading. The fading until there's nothing left but the cold pavement beneath my feet, and the absence of everything I was.

I think of the news reports. The passing notices. The deaths of people who were more than I'll ever be, who left some kind of mark. I won't even make it into the headlines. I'll be swept up, buried in the city's ceaseless churn. There won't even be an obituary. The system doesn't need me. I wasn't born to be a part of it. But then, who was? We all start as bodies, right? Flesh and blood, ready to be molded into something they can use. Some of us get lucky. The rest of us... well, we get forgotten.

And when they find my body, they'll sweep me away like the others, just another soul discarded. Another piece of the machine. And they'll forget. They'll forget about me, just like they forget about everyone else. Because that's how it works. The world moves on, no matter what. It doesn't care about the ones who fall behind.

And me? Well, I'll just be another ghost in the gutter, waiting to be forgotten.

Chapter 20: Aftermath and Reflection

The World Continues

The city moves on. It always does.

They tell you that life's a journey. It's a lie. Life is a machine. A massive, grinding, indifferent machine. You get chewed up by the gears, and then you're spit out. You can't make it stop. You can't slow it down. People run and run, they chase something, but they never know what they're chasing. They think they're running towards something. But the truth? They're running away from themselves. Always. They think they can outrun the grind, outrun the pain, the loneliness. But in the end, you're nothing but dust. A memory that fades faster than a fart in the wind. The city doesn't care. It never has.

Johnson's still out there somewhere. The cops always are, prowling like cats, stalking the edges of the streets. I used to curse him. But now, it doesn't matter. They all forget, the way you forget about a puddle in the street once it dries up. There's no justice for people like me, no moment of recognition when they find your cold body in the alley. Maybe they'll write something down in their report. But they'll forget my name before the ink's dry.

Marie. What about her? Well, she'll keep going, won't she? Filing papers. Staring at spreadsheets. Pretending that all this means something. Pretending that she means something. But she doesn't know. She doesn't know what it's like to be so far down that even the rats won't touch you. She doesn't know what it's like to live in the spaces between the cracks, to be the shadow that no one sees, but everyone steps over. She'll get on with her life, marry some good guy, have a kid or two, and forget me in the rearview mirror. It's easier that way. Forgetting's easier than remembering. People like Marie, they grow up. They move on.

But I was real. I was a part of it.

Sometimes I think about the days I spent with her. I remember the look in her eyes when she first saw me, the way she hesitated before she dropped a dollar in my cup. It wasn't pity. No, it was something else. Something a little more honest than pity. Maybe it was guilt, or maybe she was just curious. She probably saw me as just another broken thing, a casualty of this fucked-up world. But when she walked away, there was a moment—just a flash—when I thought maybe she saw something of herself in me. Maybe she thought for a second that she could be me, that she would be me if things had gone a little differently. I don't know.

And then she was gone.

Just like the others.

I wasn't the first person she walked past that day, and I won't be the last. And that's the thing, right? You think you're something special, that you matter to someone. But in the end, the world doesn't care about you. It doesn't care about your story. It doesn't care about your pain. The world will forget you as easily as it forgets the crumbs at the bottom of the subway grate. You're just a footprint in the dirt.

But I was here. I was a piece of the machine, and while I might've been nothing to them, I was something. I was part of the underbelly, the dark side of the city that keeps everything running smoothly. The homeless don't die in the streets because they're unlucky. They die because the system's designed for them to die. That's what people like Johnson don't get. They think we're all failures, that we don't try hard enough. But we're the ones who've been chewed up by the system and spit out. We're the ones who never got a fair chance, the ones who are left to rot in the corners of a world that never even noticed we existed.

Marie, like all the rest, will one day keep on walking. She'll be successful. She'll walk right past the next guy who's lying on the sidewalk with nothing but a bottle and a dream. She'll pretend she's too busy to see him, too caught up in her perfect life to notice that he's just like I was. She'll say, "That could never be me," but deep down, she knows it could. She knows it's only a matter of time before she's crushed by the same machine that crushed me. She won't see it coming, but she'll feel it when it hits. And when it does, it won't care. The city will keep moving, indifferent to her pain, just like it was indifferent to mine.

But here's the thing, and this is the one thing that no one wants to admit: I mattered. I was here. I didn't have much—just a corner, a bottle, and a lot of time to think. But I mattered, because in the cracks where the rest of the city's noise fades out, that's where you can hear the real truth. That's where you can hear the hum of existence. It's loud. It's violent. It's unrelenting. But it's there.

You think I'm bitter? Maybe I am. But I've earned it. I've earned every second of this rage. Every second of the emptiness that I felt, and the emptiness I left behind. People can walk past, forget you, ignore you, but when you've been ground down by the machine, when you've seen enough to know that the system is rigged, you can't just go back to pretending.

The world keeps turning, and all I've got left is the echo of my existence.

That's all anyone has.

So, yeah, maybe I'm dead. But I wasn't invisible. I was here.

And I will never be forgotten.

Ana's Reflection

I didn't expect the ache to creep back in. I thought it was gone, buried somewhere in the pit of me where things like Dez live—silent, invisible. But here it is again. Like an old bruise you forgot about, and then you press it, and it comes alive. Raw, throbbing.

I'm sitting in my apartment, light slanting in through the window. The city hums like it always does, like it doesn't give a shit, and I'm just here. Existing. And suddenly, Dez's face is right there, hovering over the surface of everything. His voice. That laugh. The fire he used to have—before it was swallowed up by the world.

I didn't even know when it happened. No one called. There was no email, no letter, no final anything. I didn't get a chance to see him one last time, to scream at him, or cry, or say I loved him—whatever it is people do at the end of these things. He was just gone. Just another fucking body lying in some alley, another statistic, another sad story for someone else to forget.

And here I am, pretending it doesn't hurt, pretending I'm not haunted by him, by everything he could've been, by everything he almost was. Maybe I thought I'd moved on. Maybe I thought I had. But what the hell is moving on, really? What does that even mean? Is it just pushing the memories down until they stop clawing their way to the surface?

I keep thinking about the first time I saw him, how his eyes weren't lost yet. How we'd talk, and he'd make the world seem like it could be something different. Something better. We used to make plans, big ones. He'd talk about how we'd get out of this city, out of this hole we were in. We were going to escape. Together. Like we had time. Like we could change everything, just by wanting it enough.

But there's no escape. There's no way out, is there? You can't outrun yourself. You can't outrun a city that's designed to chew you up and spit you out. You can't outrun a world that gives you nothing and then blames you for not making something of it.

I keep asking myself: What happened? When did he become that guy? The one who never showed up, who just drifted away like smoke. Was it the drugs? Was it the booze? Was it the world? Was it me? Did I stop being enough for him? Did he stop trying to be enough for himself?

I remember his hands. They were so full of life once, like they had the power to hold the world. But I couldn't save him. I couldn't fix him. I didn't have it in me. I couldn't even save myself. And I wonder if that's why he left, or maybe he was already gone before he even left me.

I still hear him sometimes. In the silence of my apartment, in the middle of the night, I hear his voice. The way he'd tell me that he was going to make it. That he was going to turn it all around. We'd talk about our dreams, our plans, like everything was still possible. We'd laugh, and everything felt real. Everything felt like it mattered.

But the truth is, it never mattered. Not in the way we wanted it to. Life didn't bend for us. It didn't give us the breaks we thought we were owed. And somewhere along the way, I started seeing him fade. Little by little, I saw the light in his eyes dim until he wasn't even the same person anymore.

I remember one night, just before it all started going downhill, he looked at me, really looked at me, like he was searching for something, and then he said, "I don't think I'm gonna make it, Ana. Not like you think."

I didn't know what he meant. I didn't know that was the last time he'd let himself be vulnerable with me. I thought he was just talking. You know how we all do when we're trying to dodge what we really mean. But I wasn't strong enough to see it for what it was. I couldn't save him. I couldn't fix him.

I keep telling myself that it wasn't my fault. But it feels like it is. Maybe if I'd been stronger. Maybe if I hadn't been so fucking caught up in my own life, my own world, I could've done something. But I didn't. I watched him slip further into himself, and I did nothing.

And now he's dead. And maybe I didn't even know him anymore. Maybe I was just holding onto an image of him, the one I wanted him to be. Maybe the truth is, I didn't love him at all. I just loved the idea of him, the promise of him.

You can't love someone for their potential forever. You can't wait for them to come back to you. They either do, or they don't. And Dez? He didn't.

It's not for him that I'm sad. It's not for the man he became. It's for the person he could've been. The man I thought he was. The man I loved, even when I didn't have the guts to say it.

The world doesn't care about people like Dez. It doesn't care about the lost, the broken, the ones who fell through the cracks. They get swept up in the noise, in the shuffle of the city, and nobody notices. Nobody remembers them once they're gone. They're just another fucking name on a pile of bodies that never made it.

I know I can't change it. I can't change him, and I can't change the way this city chews people up and spits them out. But I still think about him. I still wonder if he knew, deep down, that he could've been more. He could've been someone. And I wonder if he ever regretted it. Ever regretted giving up on us.

Maybe in the end, the only thing I'll have left is the ghost of him. And I'll carry it around, heavy as a stone, until I'm tired of it.

But I won't forget him. Not the way he was before the world broke him. Not the way he made me believe in something bigger than both of us. That's the part of him that'll stay with me. That's the part of him that mattered.

The City as a Machine

Dez is gone. And the city, she doesn't care. The air is still thick with the stench of old garbage and diesel fumes, the way it always smells after a night of rain. The same sound of feet pounding the pavement. The same tired honks of the taxis speeding past. The same cold wind that cuts through your bones like a fucking knife. It all keeps moving. The city, she never stops.

But there's something cruel about it, something almost beautiful in how easily it swallows you whole, like a machine that takes in fuel and spits out exhaust. A heartless fucking engine, programmed to keep running until it turns to rust.

You die. You disappear into the cracks in the sidewalk. And in the blink of an eye, you're just another forgotten face, swept up into the anonymity of a city that was never meant for you. You think you matter. You think you have some kind of significance. But then you're gone. And the streets keep rolling. The subway rumbles underground, the people keep walking, their heads down, eyes focused on their little machines.

It's like you were never here at all.

Maybe that's the real horror of it. Not that you die, but that you die and the world forgets you. The world forgets everything. All that pain, all those years of longing, of struggling, of existing—gone in a second. Just another body found in an alley, a name scribbled in a forgotten police report, and then... nothing.

Dez was a ghost the moment he died. A whisper carried away on the wind. And now he's a scar no one can remember.

But the machine, the city—she doesn't care.

She keeps moving. It's an empty, endless march forward, a march with no purpose, no meaning, only the cold, inevitable beat of progress. Nothing ever changes.

What's worse, I think, is the way the city mirrors you. It's not that it's cruel. It's that it doesn't care. You are but one cog in the wheel—replaceable, disposable, insignificant. And you have no say in it. You can rage against the machine, but it doesn't even *feel* you. It doesn't flinch.

In the end, it's not the machine that's cruel. It's the fact that we're born into it, stuck in it, and die in it with no say. And it doesn't care. It never cared.

Dez was just another discarded piece of trash, but you could argue, maybe, that all of us are. Maybe we all get chewed up in the gears, ground into nothing, just waiting for the day we're swallowed whole.

We think we matter. We think that somehow, in some small way, our life should count for something. That our pain, our struggles, should be seen. But the city doesn't see us. The world doesn't see us. It moves forward, indifferent, swallowing more, grinding more, throwing away more. And nothing matters.

The worst part? The machine doesn't care.

The worst part is that, somehow, neither do we.

And when it's all over, all the noise fades into the distance, like a hum you can't place.

And you're just gone. Like a blink.

Epilogue:

The city doesn't stop. It never does. Not for a moment. Not for anyone. Not even for him.

Dez is gone. His name is already slipping through the cracks, a memory diluted by the noise of traffic, the churn of the subway, the constant hum of a million lives moving in unison yet apart. There are no statues to him, no candles lit at street corners. The cold breath of the city blows through the gaps of human interaction, indifferent, unstoppable. The few who knew his name, maybe even the few who loved him, move on, filling their own voids with the next meal, the next lover, the next day.

Marie's laughter still echoes in the street where she found her peace, her escape, her clarity in life. Johnson's patrols still slice through the night, relentless, programmed to preserve order, even as the human wreckage piles up around him. His face will blur with all the others. That's how it works. That's how it always works.

But somewhere, deep in the hum of the city, Dez lingers. Not as a person, not as a memory, but as an idea. A thought that gnaws at the edge of the machine, that insists on being acknowledged, even if it's forgotten.

The truth is, the city is not just a place of steel and glass and brick. It's a factory. A factory that runs on bodies. The young ones with their fresh, shiny shoes that keep moving forward, the ones who haven't yet learned how to buckle under the weight of time. And the old ones, the worn-down ones, the ones who slip through the cracks like Dez did. All of them just parts in a machine, working or dying, but the machine keeps running. It grinds, it chews, it spits out the broken pieces.

Dez's death doesn't change the gears. It doesn't stop the machine. It doesn't even slow it down.

But maybe, just maybe, it should. Maybe if we all stopped for a second and remembered that Dez was once a man who walked these streets with his own pulse, his own hunger, his own desires—maybe the machine would falter. Maybe it would skip a beat. But we won't. We never do. The gears keep turning. And the few who cared for him, the ones who saw him as more than a discarded thing, will always be the minority. The anomaly. The outlier in a world built to forget.

Ana will go on. She will continue to play her role in this cruel, indifferent game. She will have her own children, who will find the photos. They will grow and ask questions she won't be able to answer. She'll pretend she doesn't remember, pretending she's moved on. She will. But there will always be that crack in her soul, that wound she never asked for but carries with her like a scar. Not because Dez was hers, but because he was a part of something she couldn't save. She was never meant to save him. None of us were. Not in this city.

It's not about redemption. It never was.

Dez was a part of this place. He was woven into the same fabric that binds us all. But the fabric is frayed, and the seams are coming apart, and we're all just hanging on by a thread. It's the truth of being alive in a world that couldn't care less about who we are or what we've done. The city doesn't need us. It doesn't need our dreams, our love, or our pain. It just needs us to keep moving, to keep filling the gaps, to keep making things work, even when they don't.

Dez might have been the one to break first. But every one of us is waiting for our turn. Everyone with a heart that beats a little slower, a little weaker, a little more worn. The city, indifferent and unforgiving, is a factory built for the useful, the efficient, the productive. It eats the rest of us alive.

We talk about progress. About moving forward. But forward to what? A city that doesn't know your name? A world that won't even look you in the eye? Forward to what, when you realize that the only thing moving is the machine, and the machine doesn't stop for anyone, not even for the ones it chews up and spits out like they were never there?

Dez is gone. He's just another faded name, another forgotten face in the sea of lost ones. And yet, in some way, we are all still here. Still breathing. Still trying to be seen. But the city—the machine—keeps turning.

And we are all part of it. Every one of us.

A happy death.

About Alex Telman

Alex Telman is a globally recognized spiritual healer, author, and one of the country's most read poets. With over 45 years of experience, he has dedicated his life to helping individuals break free from negative energies, trauma, and spiritual blockages. His transformative work has empowered a diverse range of clients, including celebrities, business leaders, educators, and everyday individuals, guiding them toward emotional well-being, personal growth, and spiritual fulfillment.

From an early age, Alex demonstrated extraordinary abilities to perceive and remove harmful energies and entities, a gift that first emerged when he was just three years old. This rare talent led him to study with psychic masters across the globe—Afghanistan, France, Sweden, Israel, England, and Australia—each recognizing his unique gifts and helping him refine his craft.

In addition to his healing practice, Alex has practiced as a barrister, teacher, university lecturer, and small business owner, offering a well-rounded perspective on healing that combines spirituality with practical action. He is also an accomplished author, whose writings inspire and uplift readers by exploring the depths of human emotion and the power of self-healing.

Through his sessions, Alex has helped countless individuals overcome emotional turmoil and reclaim their lives. His work transcends cultural and geographical boundaries, offering profound healing to those in need. His mission is simple yet powerful: to guide people back to their authentic selves, helping them live with purpose, peace, and fulfillment.

With a career built on compassion, wisdom, and deep spiritual insight, Alex remains a beacon of hope for anyone seeking to overcome their struggles and wanting to step into a life of clarity and joy.

Other Titles by Alex Telman

Non Fiction

Think Like a Modern Guru

Mastering Hypnosis: Complete Step-by-Step Manual, Case Studies, and Sample Scripts

From Cursed to Cured: 100 True Stories of Healing from Curses

Connecting to the Afterlife: a how-to guide

Your Journey from Death to Rebirth

Empower Your Sundays: Unlocking Inner Strength for a Resilient Life

The Truth Behind the Creation Story: A Journey Through Reincarnation

Practical Mentalism in a Nutshell

Reprogram Your Mind in a Nutshell

Meditation in a Nutshell

Alex Telman in Quotes

Novels

One Life, Half Lived

Down and Out in Byron Bay

God Speaks: A Journey Through Creation in His Own Words

Jesus Speaks: The Man Behind the Miracle in His Own Words

Poetry

Telman: The Complete Haiku 1974-2024

Echoes of September 11

Homeless in New York

Burning Echoes of Time

From Dawn to Dusk: the life cycle in sonnets

Eternal Echoes: The Tapestry of Time and the Unseen

Snapshots of People I Have Never Met

Legends and Lessons: 36 Myths Unveiled

A Measure of Time: The Eternal Voyage of Self

Ashes of Verses: Poems Burned But Not Forgotten

Reflections on Solitude: A Poetic Journey Through The Lonely Mind

Your Friendship is a Museum

Whispers to Bella

Don't miss out!

Visit the website below and you can sign up to receive emails whenever Alex Telman publishes a new book. There's no charge and no obligation.

https://books2read.com/r/B-A-YBSCC-QWVLF

BOOKS 2 READ

Connecting independent readers to independent writers.

www.ingramcontent.com/pod-product-compliance
Lightning Source LLC
LaVergne TN
LVHW050542160826
845677LV00011B/2135

9798227894670